New Corpse in Town

NEW CORPSE IN TOWN

Secret Seal Isle

Book 1

LUCY QUINN

1.

"WELL..." COOKIE JAMES sighed quietly to herself, leaning against the doorframe of the Secret Seal Inn. "I could certainly get used to this view."

But despite the fact that the inn was situated on one of the highest points on Secret Seal Isle, affording her a perfect angle on the rest of the small town spread out before her, all the way to the scenic coastline and the Atlantic Ocean beyond, that wasn't what had captured her attention.

Nor was it the porch of the same historic inn she now stood in—and owned.

Rather, her gaze lingered on the man standing on the other side of that porch, wrestling an old, rotted railing out of place. An already overheated, shirtless man with the full blaze of the late-morning sunlight glistening off the perspiration clinging to his short, dark hair—and to the finer hairs that covered most of his lean, muscular torso.

It was a very nice view indeed.

Cookie had thought she'd been quiet enough, but the man—Dylan was his name, she remembered, Dylan Creed—must have heard her, or simply felt the heat of her stare, because his own gaze lifted to catch hers. Steely blue eyes—bright enough for her to make out from here—locked with her own soft brown ones, and an impish grin flashed across his rugged features.

It was a grin that clearly said, 'Yes, I know you're looking, and I don't mind. And yes, I know you think I'm hot, and you're right.' It didn't seem to carry the usual arrogance of many attractive men, however. It was more a simple statement of fact, an acknowledgment of his own appearance, rather than a demand for praise.

Then his eyes dipped, first to Cookie's full lips, then lower, where her white button-down shirt struggled in vain to restrain the abundance of her curves. His grin widened, his stare once more returning to her own, and now she could read a different message in it: 'You can look all you want, but turnabout is fair play.'

From the gleam in his eye and the hint of desire tingeing his smile, there was an addition to that thought, one that made Cookie flush at its directness, even if she certainly didn't object to the statement: 'And I like what I see.'

With a last tug, the railing came loose, and Dylan slowly lowered it out of the way. Now Cookie had an unobstructed view of his chest, which was just as impressive as it had seemed at first glance. She tried not to linger too long, though, before returning to his face.

She'd already been caught out once—no sense making it twice in as many seconds.

"I'll have this new rail installed in a jiffy," he called out to her, his voice deep and rich with the timbre of the local Maine accent. He tilted his head for a second to study the rest of the porch, where several brand-new rails already attested to his work. "A quick coat of paint and this whole porch will look good as new."

"Thank you so much," Cookie told him honestly. "I really appreciate all your hard work."

Now he almost did look embarrassed as he shrugged. "Just doing my job," he answered. Which was true. In a town the size of Secret Seal, there was only need for one all-purpose handyman, and around here Dylan Creed was it. Whatever work you needed, if it wasn't something you could handle yourself, you called him—carpentry, plumbing, electrical work, lawn care.

She suspected he'd be happy to move furniture or help the lobstermen haul in the day's catch, if it came to that. Even after only observing him for a few minutes, Cookie could tell that he wasn't the kind of man who liked being idle.

Which was certainly good news for her and her mother, because it turned out that the Secret Seal Inn needed a lot more work than either of them had realized when they'd bought it. And neither of them was exactly handy.

At least when it came to things like woodwork.

Dylan was still watching her, she realized with a start.

"Where'd you all come in from?" he asked finally. Naturally, in a town this small, he'd have known they were new.

"Boston," she answered with a small smile. "We needed a change, just to get away from it all." Images of Boston flashed through her mind, but they were quickly replaced with scenes from Philly, the field office there, her old desk, her coworkers, the cases she'd worked… and the one that had sent her running here.

Not being privy to the dark turn her thoughts had taken, Dylan gave her a slow smile of his own. "If you wanted to get away from it all," he told her, the gravel in his voice sending a delicious shiver up her spine, "you certainly came to the right place."

She laughed to cover the thrill his words had given her. "What about you?" she asked, suddenly feeling bold. "Local boy makes good?"

That got an answering chuckle from him, deep and low and rumbling. "I guess you could say that," he replied, smile broadening. He gestured behind him, to where an old, battered truck sat in the driveway. "I've got my own wheels, my own place, and I'm my own boss. Not too shabby for a guy who was once voted 'most likely to get tossed overboard.'"

Cookie laughed with him. "I don't think we had that caption in our yearbook," she admitted. She twirled a piece of her long brown hair around her fingers and didn't miss the way Dylan's eyes darted to the movement. That thrill was back, and now it was expanding from her chest outward, sending tingles of warmth all through her that had nothing to do with the sun. She was flirting, she realized. For the first time in what felt like forever.

And she was definitely enjoying it.

"Maybe I could take you out for lunch sometime," she suggested and hastily added, "as a thank you, I mean. For all your help." Heat flushed her cheeks. It had been a long time since she'd danced this particular number.

Dylan opened his mouth to reply, but a high-pitched scream cut him off.

"Coooooooooooookkkkiiiieeeeeeeeeeee!"

Astonished, Cookie stared at him for a second, all flirtation forgotten. Where was that shrill, girlish shriek coming from? Especially one that sounded an awful lot like—

It was then that she spotted the figure racing up the hill toward her from behind the inn; back where the ground sloped away gently before ending in a short ledge a few feet above the ocean. An ocean that the running, screaming woman must have been in, judging by the water still streaming from her body. A body covered only by a pair of short jean cut-offs, Cookie realized at the same time her brain finally kicked in, confirming the woman's identity.

Oh, for the love of... the older woman was completely topless. The bouncing going on was not her personality, either.

"Mom?" Cookie was down off the porch in an

instant, hand going to the small of her back where her pistol rested beneath the loose tails of her shirt. "Mom!"

Rain raced up to her and flung her arms around Cookie, heedless of the water now soaking them both. The briny scent of the ocean filled Cookie's senses.

"Oh, Cookie." Her mother sobbed. "It was horrible. He tried to kill me!" Then, noticing Dylan for the first time, her mother paused. Switching gears instantly, Rain swept back the short, bobbed hair she had taken to dyeing a bright red and fluttered her eyelashes at him. "Well, hello there."

"Mom!" Just seconds before, Cookie had been struggling to pull free of her mother's wet embrace. Now, however, she wished they were still clenched, as she stepped between Rain and Dylan. "You're half-naked," she hissed over her shoulder.

"Oh, pshaw!" her mother replied, slapping her lightly on that same shoulder as she stepped to the side to reveal herself once again. "A good-looking man like him, I'm sure it's nothing he hasn't seen before." The smile she sent Dylan's way could have lit a grill without any need of gas or charcoal. "Though maybe not quite this nice, hm?"

And even without seeing it Cookie knew her mother was hefting her still-ample chest up for inspection. She sighed. Cookie wondered, not for the first time, why it had ever seemed like a good idea to bring her mother along.

To his credit, Dylan kept his eyes strictly at head

level, but if he felt embarrassed, shocked, or horrified it didn't show in his voice or his face. Amused, perhaps, but out of the possible list of reactions he could have had, that was far better than Cookie had expected.

"I'm sure they're lovely, ma'am," he replied, "but I have a strict 'no admiring a woman's assets before we're on a first-name basis' rule." The grin he sent Cookie's way made her flush again. She'd hired him over the phone based off a recommendation from the proprietor over at the Salty Dog, and this morning was the first time they'd met in person.

Damn it, now wasn't the time. Turning back around, she faced her mother instead. "All right, Mom, what are you talking about?" Cookie demanded, hands on her hips—and still conveniently close to her gun. "Who tried to kill you?" Because, flighty as Rain could be, that wasn't the kind of thing she'd make up.

Reminding her of her recent trauma made Rain return to panic mode. "Oh, it was terrible, sweetie," she declared, wringing her hands together. "I was just out back sunbathing, you know? And it was so nice and warm, and then the girls got a little too toasty, so I thought 'I'll just hop in the water a sec to cool off.'"

Cookie shuddered at the very idea of diving into the Atlantic. Even with the lovely mid-spring weather, the water still had to be forty degrees or less.

"And there he was!" Rain waved her hands out in front of her, the skin of her upper arms flapping around like fish out of water.

"There who was?" Cookie asked, fighting back another sigh. Interrogating suspected terrorists had been easier than this.

"The man!" Rain insisted. "The dead man. He tried to drown me!"

"Dead man?" Now Cookie was really confused. "What dead man? Where?"

"There, in the water." Her mother pointed back the way she'd come. "He was floating there in the ocean, only I didn't see him until it was too late. I landed right on top of him, and his arms wrapped around me like, well"—she winked over her shoulder at Dylan—"like any man's would. Only he was dead."

Cookie frowned. A dead man in the ocean? That was a new one. But she could see that her mother was serious. *At least it wasn't a real threat,* she thought as she let her hands drift back away from her gun. Not to them, anyway.

"We'd better call someone about it, I guess," Cookie said finally. The town had a sheriff's office—she remembered seeing it the other day when she'd been at the grocery getting supplies. They'd know what to do.

"Sounds like you'll be wanting Deputy Swan," Dylan commented. His grin was gone, all expression fled from his face as he backed away. "I'd best get out of your hair. I'll come by later to finish up with that railing."

"Oh. Okay. Sure. Thanks." Cookie watched him go, confused. For someone whose whole business was helping people with any job that needed doing, he seemed awfully eager to not offer any help now. Then again, dealing with a dead body wasn't exactly the same as repainting a door or rehanging a shutter.

Fortunately, this was one thing she actually *was* handy with.

But as he stopped to grab his T-shirt and pull it back on, Dylan caught her eye—and grinned. "I'll take a rain check on that lunch, okay?" he called.

Cookie smiled back, reassured that he hadn't totally lost interest. Maybe being around dead bodies just made him uncomfortable? She knew people like that.

Behind her, her mother thwacked her on the shoulder again. "You've already got a date with him?" she asked, and Cookie could hear the glee in Rain's voice. "How wonderful for you, sweetie. See, I told you this place would be good for us."

"Sure, Mom," Cookie agreed absently. "Now, if you'll excuse me, I'd better go call in that corpse this heavenly refuge chose to dump at our doorstep."

"Oh, don't be a Debbie Downer," her mother hollered after her, but Cookie didn't bother to respond.

2.

"**H**UH.**"** THE DEPUTY squatted near the edge of the overhang, shading his eyes from the sun even though he already had sunglasses on, and peered down at the body floating in the ocean not four feet away. "You're right, he looks dead."

"Gee, d'ya think?" Cookie snapped from where she crouched, an arm's length away. "What was your first clue, that he's facedown in the water or that he's not moving—or breathing?"

She'd come down here to study the body herself right after she'd called the sheriff's office, but had been careful not to touch it. Which meant, of course, that she couldn't turn the corpse over or check his pockets. Right now all she knew for certain was that the deceased was most likely male, Caucasian, roughly six feet tall, neither cadaverous nor overweight, and possessed a full head of dark hair. She suspected he'd been in the water at least a day, judging from the pale, wrinkled nature of what skin she could see at his wrists and neck. But he'd also acquired a hefty collection of seaweed somewhere along the way, which had clumped onto the corpse, making it difficult to discern any other details.

Water lapped at the dock as she waited for the deputy to offer any other commentary, but her patience—which had never been her strong suit and was already frayed by the very fact that there was a body, and it was behind her inn, and her mother was the one who had found it—was fading fast.

"Well?" she urged finally when the deputy still hadn't moved.

He turned to glance over at her. "I'll radio the sheriff," he said slowly, "and have her send the ME to collect the body. We'll get him out of your way in no time." With that he stood, dusting off his pant legs, and adjusted his sunglasses.

But Cookie wasn't done. "That's it?" she asked, following the deputy as he retraced his steps around the inn toward the front where his cruiser was parked. "I'm not worried about having a body cluttering up the water by my back porch, Deputy," she pointed out. "A man's dead here. Something has to be done about that."

Deputy Swan—whose only resemblance to his namesake was the way he waddled when he walked—stopped and studied her. "What exactly is it you want us to do, Ms. James?" he asked.

"I want you to investigate!" she all but yelled. She managed to regain her composure and said, "That's what you do when someone gets killed. You find out how it happened, and why, and if somebody's responsible."

Swan pulled off his sunglasses and rubbed at one cheek where the frames had rested. Without the mirrored shields over his eyes, he looked surprisingly young, most likely early twenties, with baby fat still visible in his round, fleshy face. "Responsible?" he said now, his eyebrows rising toward the heavy mass of his black hair. "Most likely he got drunk, tripped, and fell into the water and drowned. Then the ocean washed him up here, which is just our bad luck but nothing more."

"Bad luck?" Cookie stared at the local lawman. "He's the one who's dead." She flashed back to what he'd just said. "Wait, so you're saying he's not even local? How do you know?"

Deputy Swan sighed. "Ma'am, I know because with the welcome addition of you and your lovely mother, Secret Seal Isle has exactly 347 people, every one of which I know on sight—and he ain't one a' them." He shook his head. "Which means he's from the mainland somewhere. So he ain't really my problem."

Cookie bit back another angry retort. She'd already been dismayed when the baby-faced deputy had arrived and she'd asked if the sheriff would be following soon. "Sheriff?" Deputy Swan had replied. "Ma'am, Sheriff Watkins is over in Hancock. I'm the only deputy assigned this island, and she won't come out here or send anybody else 'less I ask for backup."

How could an entire island not have its own police force? Cookie had wondered, and still did. Okay, sure, the island's whole population would probably fit in one high school auditorium. And yes, Secret Seal Isle hardly seemed like a bastion of criminal activity or unrestrained violence. It irked her nonetheless. As did Deputy Swan's rather cavalier attitude toward the whole thing.

As if reading her mind, Swan laid a heavy hand on her shoulder. "I wouldn't worry about it," he assured her. "Like I said, mainland problem. I suggest you go about your business." Then he crossed to his car, tipped his head in her direction, and quickly climbed into the driver's seat.

He hadn't bothered to lock the door, Cookie noted.

She watched the deputy drive away, her fists clenched as she fumed silently.

"WELL, HE DIDN'T seem too concerned," Rain offered, the chain of the hammock squeaking as she swung. She'd covered her exposed chest, thank goodness, and had stayed on the inn's front porch the entire time, delivering her statement as quickly as possible. Then she'd retreated to the hammock slung from hooks at the far end. Cookie's mother had never been terribly comfortable with lawmen. "Too many raids when I was young," she'd once explained.

"No, he didn't," Cookie agreed, resisting the urge to lash out at her mother just because she was the only one around. "But if a whole group of armed men were sighted just off the shore in a boat packed with Stinger missiles, he'd probably tell us 'don't worry, they won't bother us none' and leave it at that." She stared down the hill, where she could still see the deputy's car making its leisurely way toward the sheriff's office, then looked toward the backyard, the water, and the body it contained. The body Deputy Swan clearly couldn't be bothered with.

But it was bothering her. And that made her want to bother someone else about it.

There were plenty of reasons she shouldn't, Cookie knew. Not least of which was the fact that she and her mother had come here—fled here, if she was being honest—to get away from it all. To hide. To lie low. Calling people now would be the exact opposite of that.

But a man was dead. And, local or not, that wasn't something she could just let go.

Having made her decision, Cookie acted upon it. Gliding past her mother, who had risen from the hammock to hover near the inn's front door, Cookie headed inside and up the stairs, the wooden steps cool on her bare feet. The second and third floors were for guests. And her mother had claimed the lone bedroom on the main floor, opposite the front parlor, dining room, and kitchen, but Cookie had set her sights on one of the two rooms nestled into the attic. Making her way up there now, she opened the door, and heat from the sun wafted toward her as she eased inside. She made a mental note to check on those window air-conditioning units she'd ordered.

The room was good-sized, though a taller person might have had issues with the way the ceiling sloped in along the front. At 5'9", Cookie didn't mind at all. She thought it made the room seem cozy, and besides, she loved the big dormer window that took up most of that wall, looking out toward the water. But at the moment, she wasn't interested in the view. Instead she slid between her bed and dresser and went to the small closet. It was stuffed with clothes, but her goal was actually a small strongbox tucked away on the top shelf. She had to strain on her tiptoes to get her fingers on it, and it scraped on the wooden shelf as she gingerly pulled it toward her until she could grab it properly and haul it down.

Setting the box on the bed, Cookie unlocked it with a key she kept in her pocket. Then, taking a deep breath, she flipped the lid open and sat staring at her past.

It was strange that so much of one's life could fit into so compact a space, she thought, gazing down at the box's contents. Or perhaps the word she was looking for was "sad." Certainly some of her old friends, especially her best friend, Scarlett, had told her she needed to get a life. Maybe this just proved their point.

Shaking off the doldrums those old memories brought forth, Cookie dug into the box, looking for what she needed. Past the holstered pistol, beneath the badge and ID, under passport and birth certificate and diplomas—aha! She snatched up the item and held it to the light like a long-lost prize.

"Oh, how I've missed you," she murmured affectionately.

Then she popped it open, slapped the battery into place, shut it back up, and then powered the phone on.

Its starting chime was a welcome note that almost brought tears to her eyes. When they'd left Philly, she and Rain had agreed that they needed to break all ties with their past. That included ditching or hiding anything people could have used to reach them. Rain had happily discarded her own phone, but Cookie had found she just couldn't bear to get rid of hers. Instead it had been placed in the box, powered off but still available in case she needed it.

As she did right now.

Once the phone lit up, Cookie was relieved to see that it was showing full bars. She hadn't been sure the island even had cell service, and they were too far from the mainland to access any signal from there. Cookie called up her contacts list, scrolling down to a particular name. One she'd thought she'd never see again.

Then, after taking another deep breath for strength, she hit Call.

3.

H E PICKED UP on the second ring.

"Charlie?" he demanded, his voice the same deep, gruff rumble she remembered. "Are you okay? Where the hell are you?" She could hear the naked concern in his voice, but also the anger.

This wasn't going to be easy.

"I'm... okay," Cookie managed after a second, gripping the phone tightly. "Really. I just... we had to get out."

That made him pause, and when he spoke again some of the anger had been tamped down. "Yeah, I get that," he admitted. "I do. But you could've told me, Charlie. I'd have helped." Now the anger had been replaced by, of all things, hurt, and Cookie found herself blinking back tears. Damn. This wasn't how this was supposed to go.

"I know," she answered, regret in her tone. "I do. But it was better to not involve anybody else. Once I made the decision, we just packed up and ran." Even though it had meant throwing away everything she'd worked for all these years. Leaving behind her entire career, her friends… and her partner. After she'd tangled with a mob family and lost, she'd opted to take an unspecified extended leave from her job at the FBI… otherwise known as a career killer. But she'd had no other choice if she wanted to protect herself and her mother.

"I tried calling, you know," he said. "A whole bunch of times. No answer. Tried pinging your phone, too. Nothing."

She had to laugh at that. "Did you really think I wouldn't know how to avoid that?" she asked. "Come on, Hunter—you taught me better than that."

"Yeah, I guess I did." He chuckled as well, the same warm, liquid sound that had always sent more of a thrill through her than it probably should. "So, what do you need? I'm guessing you didn't resurface just to check in."

"No." Cookie sighed. "I—this thing happened. Nothing to do with me, not exactly, but it was right on my doorstep—pretty much literally—and the local deputy isn't exactly eager to look into it."

"And you can't, because you're not in the game anymore, officially," Hunter guessed. "So, what, you want me to come out there and check it out for you?"

"Would you?" She held her breath as she stared blindly at her patchwork quilt. She knew it was a lot to ask, especially after she'd gone dark on him.

"Just tell me where you are," her former partner answered, allowing Cookie to breathe again as relief and gratitude flowed over her in a wave. "I'll be on the next flight out."

OF COURSE, IT wasn't quite as simple as just hopping a plane. One of the most appealing features of Secret Seal Isle was its remoteness, since Cookie and Rain hadn't exactly wanted to make it easy for anyone to find them. Which was why it wasn't until the next day that Hunter showed up.

He'd already missed the body. Not that it hadn't been there long enough. Cookie didn't know if Deputy Swan had called his boss back in Hancock or had just finally found a little initiative of his own. Or maybe he'd just decided that leaving a body floating right off their blissful little island could ruin its tourist appeal or foul the lobstermen's nets or something else equally heinous. But someone had finally gotten around to notifying the medical examiner, because the white van arrived early the next morning, with 'Hancock Medical Examiner's Office' emblazoned on the side.

Cookie had hung back while the ME, a tall, thin, geeky Hispanic guy who looked too young for the job, had wrestled the body out of the water and into a body bag, which he'd then hauled back to the van and carted off. The island didn't have a hospital or medical center, so she assumed he would be taking the ferry back to the mainland.

The other big event that morning had been the

arrival of their first paying guests. Mary and Henry Seiger were from New Jersey, and they had decided to have a romantic getaway to celebrate their thirtieth wedding anniversary. They'd heard of Secret Seal Isle somewhere and had booked their weeklong trip through the new online reservations system. Cookie was thrilled, both because the older couple seemed nice and provided a welcome distraction and because the whole idea of buying the inn had been so they could earn a living, and that required guests.

She'd just finished showing the Seigers their room— the largest one on the second floor, with a beautiful bay window and a lovely view of the island and the ocean— when a rental car pulled up in front. A Mustang, new and gleaming black, as if it'd been torn from the night itself.

And out of the car had stepped a man just as dark and masculine as his ride.

"Hunter!" Cookie's feet pounded on the wooden porch steps as she raced down and all but threw herself at him. Fortunately, at six feet and fit, with well-honed muscles, Hunter was able to take the impact. She laughed as he swept her up into his arms, lifting her right off her feet. "You made it."

"Finally. I'm amazed, too," her ex-partner admitted, squeezing her tight before setting her down. Frustration and amusement warred in his dark eyes. "Do you have any idea what a pain it is to get here from Philly?" He stopped and shook his head. "Of course you do," he corrected himself. "You did this yourself. And that was part of the point, right?" He laughed again, running one hand over his gleaming scalp. "Well, let me tell you, mission accomplished. No way are any of DeMasi's crew ever finding you out here—and even if they did, none of them would be willing to make the trip."

Though hearing the mob boss's name again made her shiver a little, Cookie was pleased that Hunter agreed with her choice of hideaway. And she was just really glad to see him. "You look good," she said, studying him. His beard was still neatly trimmed, his head shaved bare, his dark suit perfectly pressed. Hunter O'Neil had always been the poster child for the FBI's sexy-but-dangerous-agent type.

He'd been doing his own studying, of course, and now a small, sexy smile tugged at the corner of his mouth. "You too," he said softly, his eyes sliding over her curves and leaving a tingle of heat in their wake. "Looks like hiding out agrees with you."

Cookie could feel herself flush. "It's not so bad. At least I don't have to wear a suit anymore," she cracked, waving a hand at her untucked button-down shirt and jeans.

"You always looked good in a suit," Hunter replied, his gaze heating up further. "Though you look darn good out of it, too."

Fortunately, Rain chose just that moment to emerge from the inn. "Oh, hello!" she called out, tripping down the steps toward them. "I'm Cookie's mother, Rain. And who might you be?"

At least, Cookie thought, *she's wearing a top this time.*

Hunter arched one eyebrow but smiled and offered his hand. "Hunter O'Neil," he answered. "Your daughter and I used to work together."

"Oh?" Rain turned toward her daughter, and over her shoulder Hunter mouthed, *Cookie?* Cookie just shook her head and gave an 'I'll explain later' shrug. "Sweetie," her mom was saying now, "you never told me about a coworker named Hunter." What Rain really meant, Cookie knew from her wide grin, was 'you never mentioned you worked with such a hottie.'

"There's a lot I didn't tell you, Mom," Cookie managed quietly, and for once her mom just nodded, not pushing her on it. "Hunter came up because of what happened yesterday."

"Oh, it was horrible!" Rain declared at once, going back into drama mode like the flip of a switch. "He was all over me. I was practically peeing myself, I was so scared." Then the switch tripped again, and she was all smiles. "Will you be staying with us, Hunter?" she practically cooed up at him. "You simply must."

"If I must, I must," Hunter agreed easily.

"Oh, good." Rain clapped her hands together like a little girl who'd just been allowed a treat. "And I know the perfect room for you. I'll go get it ready." Turning away from him, she leaned in close to Cookie and whispered, "He's hotter than a pig roast in July."

Cookie managed not to groan or roll her eyes, but

only barely, as her mother skipped away.

"Okay," Hunter said once they were alone again. "Obviously I want to hear what exactly happened yesterday. But first—Cookie? Rain?" He was laughing at her, of course, but Cookie couldn't find it in herself to be offended. Especially not when it really was so ridiculous.

"I couldn't go by my real name," she explained, "just in case Jonah did have someone looking for me." She shrugged. "When I was a kid, my nickname was Cookie because I loved the darn things. It's familiar enough that I actually answer to it, and it's not listed on anything anywhere, so it seemed like the best option."

"I get that," he agreed. "But—Rain?"

Now Cookie did laugh as she led him toward the inn. "What can I say? Mom's still an old hippie at heart. She figured if I was changing my name, she might as well change hers too, and she said she'd always thought Mary was boring. So she became Rain Forest instead."

"Wow." He laughed again. "Rain Forest? Really? That's—I just can't picture you growing up with a mom named Rain Forest." Then he sobered. "All right, now tell me what happened yesterday."

Cookie found herself bringing him to the dock and recounting the incident with the dead body and her encounter with Deputy Swan. "They hauled off the body this morning," she finished, "but there isn't even so much as crime scene tape. No forensics, no photos, nothing."

"We're not in the big city anymore," Hunter pointed

out. "They do things differently around here." He tugged on the legs of his suit pants as he squatted down and inspected the area where they'd discovered the body. He chuckled again. "But I take it that's not good enough for you."

"The deputy wasn't concerned because the man wasn't local, but he's still dead," Cookie shot back, squinting at him in the fading light. "And I think, whoever the hell he is, he deserves for people to know what happened to him, and how, and why."

Hunter considered that, rubbing his jaw, before standing up and finally nodding. "Okay," he said. "You're right. A man's dead, and somebody's got to find out the details and make sure anyone responsible is brought to justice." He yawned and stretched before he looked at his watch. "It's after five, and I'm betting Deputy Swan doesn't exactly stay late. How about we pick this up in the morning—go talk to him, see what he can tell us, and take it from there? In the meantime, all that traveling wore me out. I could use a good meal, a beer, and a solid night's sleep."

Cookie smiled. "I think we can provide those, no problem." She gestured grandly toward the inn. The back door was standing open invitingly, the light from inside casting a warm glow out onto the deck even as the sky darkened around them. "After all, you're staying at the finest inn on Secret Seal Isle."

It was also the *only* inn on the island, but she decided her ex-partner didn't need to know that.

"THAT WAS EXCELLENT, ma'am," Hunter said. His chair scraped on the old hardwood floor as he pushed back from the dinner table, dabbing at his mouth with his napkin. "Thank you."

Rain beamed down at him. "My pleasure," she replied. "And it's Rain." She slapped at him playfully before reaching over and scooping up his empty plate. "Cookie, sweetie, why don't you show Hunter to his room?" she suggested with a wink. "I put him in Borealis."

Cookie groaned. She loved her mother dearly, but the woman didn't have a subtle bone in her body. Still, now wasn't the time to get into it with her. "Come on," she told Hunter, rising to her feet. "It's on the top floor."

Hunter hoisted the duffel he'd pulled from his rental car and followed her up the stairs. "Why'd you groan when your mom told you which room it was?" he asked as they climbed. "Something wrong with the room?"

"Not at all," Cookie answered over her shoulder, breathing a little heavily from the steep ascent. "It's just—" She reached the top floor and paused to catch her breath before stepping to the side so Hunter could join her. "This is Borealis," she continued, reaching out and opening one of the three doors.

Hunter stepped into the room, tastefully decorated with northern lights prints, distressed furniture, and a white goose-down comforter. He surveyed it quickly. "Nice." He tossed his duffel onto the bed.

"Yeah. And that's the bathroom." She pointed toward the middle door. Then she indicated the remaining door. "And this is Aurora. My room."

"Ah." A devilish look kindled in Hunter's eyes. "So your mom put me in the room next to yours? And we're the only ones up here?"

"That's about the size of it." Cookie tried to meet his eyes but found she had to look away from the heat there. "Well, good night."

She turned away, but Hunter shot out a hand and caught her by the wrist. "Hey, not so fast," he urged. "It's not all that late, and I don't know about you, but I don't have anywhere I need to be. Maybe we can… catch up?" His thumb stroked the inside of her wrist, sending delicious shivers up her arm and all through her body. "Hang out?" His voice had dropped, becoming even deeper, and that too was making her quiver in all the right ways. "Get reacquainted?"

Cookie could feel herself melting all over. There was no denying it—she'd always been a little bit in love with her hot, sexy, dangerous partner. And she'd always thought that maybe, just maybe, there'd actually been something real behind the way he'd flirted with her. But they'd been partners, and neither of them had been willing to jeopardize that.

But they weren't partners anymore.

Still, she found that she didn't want to just jump into bed with him. Or, rather, she did—she really did—but she also knew that probably wasn't the best idea.

Especially when he'd just arrived, and she was still getting used to being here. And there was this whole dead-body thing to deal with.

She disengaged her wrist and stepped back. "I think maybe we should both sleep on it," she suggested gently. "Let's see how things look in the morning."

Hunter opened his mouth as if he was going to argue, but then he nodded instead. "You're right, it's late. I'm tired and probably not at my best. Tomorrow, though." He leveled a finger at her, along with a gaze that should by rights have made her clothes burst into flames. "We're not done with this conversation."

Then he slipped into his room and eased the door shut behind him with a soft click.

Cookie stared at his door, fanning herself.

Well, crap, she thought as she turned toward her own room. She had a feeling she was going to have a hard time getting to sleep now.

But when she did, she suspected the dreams would be worth the wait.

4.

"**O**KAY, YOU TWO lovebirds, sorry to wake you, but—oh!" Rain's cheery singsong voice cut through the last of Cookie's dreams, dragging her kicking and screaming back up to the bright light of early morning. She dragged the quilt off her head and blinked blearily through the tangle of her dark hair. Her mother was peering down at her, looking confused.

"Whuzzat?" Cookie demanded, reaching up to brush her hair from her face so she could see more clearly.

"Where is that fine, fine man of yours?" Rain demanded, hands going to her hips. Over her tie-dyed peasant top and short-shorts she was wearing an apron that insisted *Kiss the Cook!* in big, bold letters. "Don't tell me you sent him back to his own room after you had your way with him last night."

"My way with what? Huh?" Cookie was the first to admit that she'd never been a morning person. Back in Philly, she'd never owned a coffee machine because it was a cruel irony that she had no chance of figuring out how to work one of the darn things without at least one cup of coffee in her. Now she tried to kick-start her brain back into gear so she could make sense of what her mother was saying.

Finally, it clicked. "Oh. Oh!" She sat up straight. "Hunter's in his room, I'm guessing. I have no idea. But that's where he went after we came upstairs last night. Him to his room, me to mine." She frowned at her mother. "No thanks to you."

"What?" Rain actually had the audacity to look insulted. "You mean to tell me you wasted a perfectly good night and an incredibly hot man just a few feet from your bed? Charlene Esmeralda Jamieson, I'm ashamed of you!"

It is way too early to deal with my mother's twisted logic, Cookie thought with a groan as she rubbed both palms against her eyelids. "Aren't you supposed to be telling me *not* to sleep around?" she asked, hating the fact that her voice came out in a half whine. "I'd ask if this was reverse psychology, but sadly I know better."

"Reverse nothing," Rain replied. "That man is hot, hot, hot, and you know it. And the way he was looking at you, like he wanted to just eat you up with a spoon…" She sighed. "Oh, I'd give a lot to have a man like that look at me that way again."

"Mom!" Now Cookie wanted to rub her eyes again, not to wake up further but to try scrubbing away that mental image. "Hunter's my ex-partner. And my friend. We were never anything more."

"Well, that's your own damn fault," her mother retorted, turning back toward the door. "And if I were you, I'd do something to fix that, and soon, before he heads back to Philly." She paused in the hall. "Oh, and breakfast will be ready in ten."

"At last, some good news," Cookie grumbled, climbing out of bed. The morning air was cool on her skin, and she had goose bumps when she staggered out into the hall.

And almost ran smack into Hunter.

"Morning," he said with just the touch of a grin. He was wearing a T-shirt that hugged every muscle and a pair of sweatpants. Perspiration glistened across his scalp and dampened his shirt. It was clear he'd just come back from a morning run.

"Morning," Cookie replied, all too aware that her hair was a mess, she had no makeup on, and she was wearing nothing but panties and an oversized T-shirt with the collar cut out. "Um, breakfast is in ten. I'll be right down." She scooted past him to the bathroom, diving inside as if it were shelter from a raging storm, and practically slamming the door shut behind her.

She could swear she felt Hunter's gaze tracking her the whole way, its touch on her almost-exposed skin searing her right through the sleep shirt.

The water at the inn took a while to warm up, which meant when she turned on the shower Cookie was inundated with ice-cold water.

For once, she didn't mind.

"WELCOME BACK TO the land of the living," Hunter told her when she finally made her way down to the dining room and plopped into the chair across from him. She was feeling far more human now that she'd showered, brushed her hair, and pulled on jeans, a blouse and a loose-knit sweater. Mary and Henry were seated at the other end of the long oak table, and plates of steaming food covered the center of the table between them.

"Thanks." Cookie grabbed a serving fork and shoveled a pile of pancakes onto her plate. She doused them in maple syrup then added fresh berries and real whipped cream before taking a big bite. The flavor barely registered as she worked at filling her belly. She was still chewing as she reached for the carafe and poured herself piping-hot coffee. Without hesitating, she took a big gulp to wash down the food, ignoring the searing sensation in her esophagus.

Hunter's plate was still half-full, but he paused to watch her eat. "You always could put it away," he said with a chuckle, but the twinkle in his eye showed that it wasn't a dig. "It's good, too. Your mom's one hell of a cook."

"I know," Cookie agreed around another mouthful. Truth be told, she was pretty decent in the kitchen herself, but Rain had a real flair for it, and baking too. That was why it had made perfect sense for her to handle the cooking at the inn. Plus, Cookie had hoped that stashing Rain in the kitchen might keep her out of trouble. But no such luck.

"What's our plan?" Cookie asked after she'd cleared her plate and drained her cup. She was debating if she wanted seconds of either, but at least food and coffee were no longer a burning need. Now they were just a mild desire, and she knew she'd probably resist the temptation. While Hunter was right about her being able to eat, she still tried not to overdo it. It wasn't as if she were chasing perps down the sidewalk for exercise anymore.

Hunter shrugged. "You wanted me to look into it," he reminded her, setting his napkin beside his plate. "So introduce me to the deputy, and I'll look. I can't promise anything else until I know what's going on."

Cookie nodded and wiped her mouth with her own napkin before rising and tossing it onto the chair she'd just vacated. "Let's go."

"This looks promising," Hunter commented as they approached the sheriff's office. They'd walked rather than driving. It wasn't that far—the entire town could be traversed in forty minutes, and the office was right in the center. Plus, it was a nice day out, warm but with a pleasantly cool, salty breeze off the water. It was exactly the kind of weather that made Cookie glad they'd moved here, and she didn't want to waste it by being cooped up in a car. Hunter didn't seem to mind, and they'd strolled in companionable silence, just enjoying the sunshine and the fresh air.

Cookie considered the office now herself. It did present well, she had to agree—big enough to have some gravitas but small enough to say, 'Yes, we can handle crime, but that doesn't mean we see a lot of it.' It was also old enough to look established but still clean and well maintained, with weathered brick, large windows, and an inviting glass door that certainly wouldn't hide any secrets. Still, she thought of Deputy Swan and warned, "Looks can be deceiving."

Together they pushed through the door and into the office. There wasn't a reception desk—inside, it was basically just one big room with a glassed-in office in the back and a door beside it that she guessed led to holding cells. Swan was the only person there, and he was sitting at his desk, feet up, reading the paper and sipping coffee. If he'd noticed their entrance, he didn't let on.

"Come on." Cookie led the way past empty desks to the glass office, where she rapped on the wall even though the door was open. "Deputy Swan?"

That got his attention, and he glanced up, a polite smile on his face. "Ms. James, what can I do for you?" Then his gaze skipped over to Hunter in his dark suit and sunglasses. Suddenly the chair rattled, and Swan was sitting up straight, feet flat on the floor. "Can I help you?" he asked, his voice shaking slightly.

"Special Agent Hunter O'Neil, FBI," Hunter introduced himself, pulling out his badge and ID and handing them to the deputy, who examined them with what looked like awe before passing them back. "Ms. James asked me to stop in and see how the investigation was going."

"Investigation?" Deputy Swan darted his gaze back and forth between Cookie and Hunter, clearly trying to figure out the connection there. "What investigation is that?"

Even behind his mirrored shades Cookie could see Hunter's eyebrow arch. "The dead body?" he reminded Swan. "The one found behind Ms. James's property? The one her mother stumbled onto—literally?"

"Oh, right, that." Swan gulped. "Chip Winslow."

"Wait, what?" Cookie gaped at him. "The dead guy is Chip Winslow? You said there was no way he was local!"

Now Hunter was the one whose eyes were bouncing back and forth. "You know the deceased?" he asked, his tone somewhere between hard-nosed interrogator and concerned friend.

"Everybody around here knows Chip Winslow," Cookie confirmed, "including us, and we've only been here a few weeks." She continued to glare at the deputy. "You said you didn't recognize him."

"I didn't! I can't be expected to remember every person who steps onto this rock." Swan protested, his voice rising as his face reddened. "The ME called with the ID just a few minutes ago." He lifted his chin. "And Chip Winslow isn't local. He just wants—wanted—to be."

Hunter made a sound in the back of his throat, half cough and half growl. "Somebody want to tell me who this Winslow character was?"

Cookie sighed. "All I know is he's from the area, at least New England, and probably Maine if not the island itself. He's rich, and he had all these crazy plans for Secret Seal Isle. Wanted to turn it into the next Martha's Vineyard or something." She shook her head. "Last I heard, he was trying to buy the Salty Dog." Noticing the questioning look on her ex-partner's face, she explained, "It's the local sandwich shop, and yes, the only one on the island. Great place, really good food, amazing lobster rolls. It's practically the heart of the town, and Chip wanted to buy it, gut it, rip out its soul, and turn it into some crappy tourist trap."

Hunter looked to Swan, who nodded his confirmation of that assessment. "Sounds like the kind of man who isn't well-liked," Hunter commented. "The kind who has a whole lot of enemies."

The deputy was staring at him. "What, you think there was foul play?" he asked. "People slip and drown all the time, especially when there's a storm. He fell in the water, swallowed a lungful or two, passed out and drowned, and the current carried him out here. That's it."

Now Hunter slid past Cookie and slapped his hands on the desk so that he could lean across, staring down at the terrified deputy. "Do you really think that's what happened?" he asked, his voice going low and gravelly.

"That this man, who was known and hated throughout town, just happened to slip and fall and drown? And then wash up here? Just a strange, sad little coincidence?"

Swan gulped. "We're a nice, quiet place," he answered, his voice barely more than a squeak. "We don't get violence and foul play and all that out here."

Hunter straightened up. "I'd say you've got it now." He studied the deputy again, frowning. "I think I'll stick around and take over the investigation," he decided out loud. "If the murder really did happen elsewhere, this crime could have crossed state borders, which automatically makes it FBI jurisdiction." He speared Swan with a tight, wolfish smile. "You don't mind, do you?"

The overwhelmed deputy shook his head. "It's all yours," he answered and looked genuinely pleased at that thought. Which made sense, seeing as how he'd clearly not wanted anything to do with this death in the first place.

Disgust coiled in Cookie's gut. The deputy was a true disgrace to the uniform.

Then Swan's eyes slid past Hunter to Cookie. "What about her?" he asked. "She's not FBI—is she?"

"No, she's just a concerned citizen," Hunter replied, not even bothering to glance her way. "She has every right to be concerned, considering where the body was found, but she's not part of this investigation." Now he did turn toward Cookie. "Thank you for your help, ma'am," he told her without even the slightest hint of a smile. "If I need anything further, I know where to find you."

"You know… if you need…" Cookie echoed, so mad she was practically spitting. "Let's go!" she finally managed, latching onto Hunter's arm and dragging him back out into the main office toward the front door. Swan watched them, clearly puzzled but amused.

"What the hell?" Cookie demanded once she thought they were out of earshot from the deputy. "I bring you into this, and now you're gonna cut me out?"

Hunter sighed and removed his shades. "Look, Charlie," he started, "what I said in there is absolutely true as far as he's concerned. You're supposed to be a civilian now, like everybody else, right? You don't want to trust that creep with your FBI status do you? The whole point was to lay low. So, yeah, you can't get involved in this—or more involved, I guess. You came here to hide out, stay out of trouble, and not get noticed. How do you think digging into some local hotshot's murder is going to work with all that?"

What he said made sense, but Cookie was still fuming. He'd casually dismissed her and treated her like a civilian when she'd once been his right-hand man—or woman. The one who'd had his back more times than she could count. "He washed up in my backyard," she snapped. "My mom stumbled onto the body. I called you!"

"I know," Hunter said, his voice assuming that soothing cadence it always did when he was trying to calm and cajole a reluctant informant or a panicked witness. "And I promise I'll keep you apprised of what I find. But you can't be here, Charlie. You know that." He rested his hands on her shoulders, and the warmth was a little too nice as he gazed down into her eyes. "You asked me to take care of this. Let me do that. Okay?"

Cookie growled and pulled away. She could tell she wasn't going to get anywhere by arguing, though. Not right now. Hunter was like a wall—once he'd made up his mind you could try chipping away, but it was going to be slow going at best. Better to let things sit and cool down a little, then try again.

Which didn't make it sting any less as she stormed out, back onto the street. Alone and out of the loop.

Suddenly, the day that had started out so sunny and promising, now looked as cold, gray, and unpleasant as her mood.

5.

B Y THE TIME Cookie got back to the inn, the breakfast table had been cleared, Mary and Henry were nowhere to be found, and Rain was lounging in one of the porch hammocks, reading another one of her beloved romance novels. "Where have you been?" she asked, barely glancing up from the book. "And where's that stud of yours?"

"Back at the sheriff's office, and he's definitely not mine!" Cookie snapped, still furious. Her mother raised an eyebrow at the outburst but wisely chose not to pursue what was clearly a touchy subject. Just then the phone rang—not Cookie's cell, which she'd reflexively pocketed after calling Hunter the other day and was still carrying now, but the inn's landline. "I got it," Cookie announced, breezing past Rain and heading inside.

The phone was only on its third ring when she snatched up the receiver. "Secret Seal Inn, the loveliest bed and breakfast on the island, how may I help you?" she rattled off, hoping that being out of breath made her sound busy and breathless with excitement instead of asthmatic or just plain creepy.

The laugh on the other end was warm and deep, and it scattered her anger like a dog racing into a flock of pigeons. "It helps that you're the only bed and breakfast on the island," the caller added, "but I won't tell if you won't."

Cookie discovered with some surprise that she was smiling. The plastic of the phone was slick in her hand when she gripped it a little tighter. "Dylan. Hi." She didn't know what else to say.

Fortunately, he seemed eager to do the talking. "Hey yourself. I just wanted to see how you were doing. You know, after the whole dead-body thing. Because that can throw anybody off their game."

She giggled and immediately castigated herself for it. *Way to sound like a flighty bimbo,* she scolded herself silently. But it was just so nice to hear from him—and especially for him to call and be concerned and sympathetic after she'd just had to deal with Mr. Macho himself. "I'm doing okay," she admitted once she was sure her voice was steady again. "Thanks. How about you?"

"You mean the way I lit out of there?" She could hear his sigh. "Sorry about that. I'm not Swan's biggest fan, so I figured it'd be best if I wasn't around when he showed up."

"Oh?" Cookie perked up. "Did you get in too much trouble as a kid? Little juvenile delinquent Dylan, constantly running from the law?"

That got another chuckle out of him, and Cookie was quickly finding his laugh horribly addictive. "Something like that." His voice dropped a notch. "Tell you what. Buy me that lunch you promised, and maybe I'll tell you about it."

She didn't even have to think twice about that one. "Done." A quick glance at the handsome old grandfather clock in the hall told her it was just past eleven. "How's noon at the Salty Dog?"

"Noon is great. I'll see you there." He hung up, and after the click Cookie just stood there with the receiver against her cheek. Reality broke through her trance, and she returned it to its cradle before she bolted for her room. She had less than an hour to get ready.

In the end, she'd settled for just freshening up. After all, this wasn't really a date or anything—it was only lunch. And this was Secret Seal Isle, where if you wore slacks people might think you were putting on airs. So Cookie simply brushed her hair again, applied fresh lip gloss, checked for mascara flakes, and headed out.

She'd told Hunter that the Salty Dog was basically the heart of the town, and it was true. Geographically, however, it was down near the lower edge of the island, while the inn was closer to the top. They were basically on either end of town, which was why it took her almost forty minutes to get there. She'd briefly considered driving but had decided that was just silly. Nobody really used cars around here—they were primarily for use on the mainland. Here people either biked or walked. Or sailed.

The Salty Dog was right on the shore, its back end opening onto a broad, private pier set up with tables and chairs for outdoor dining when the weather was good. The day had cleared and was once again sunny and pleasant, which was why Cookie wasn't surprised to find Dylan already sitting at one of the tables outside when she arrived.

"Sorry," she said as she reached him. Cookie sank into the sun-heated plastic chair opposite him as he waved off the apology.

"You're probably on time," he pointed out. "I just came over early. Figured I could sit and relax until you got here."

"And now that I'm here you can't relax?" she teased, leaning forward a little.

Dylan eyed her carefully. "I don't know," he admitted, still smiling. "I'm not sure yet if you're one of those women who just waits for a guy to let his guard down so she can pounce."

"Would it be so bad if I was?" Cookie shot back, and then blushed when she heard herself. Oh, wow. She couldn't remember the last time she'd been this much of a flirt.

Still, it didn't look as if Dylan minded. "'Bad' isn't the word that comes to mind," he said, his smile widening.

A waiter came over, and water and menus thumped

down as he dropped them off. Cookie took advantage of the distraction, sipping at her drink to help her cool down.

Of course she already knew what she was getting—the Salty Dog was famous for its lobster rolls for a reason. Still, the menu provided a good pause for her to regain her composure and dial it down a little.

"So you've lived here your whole life?" she asked after the waiter had returned and taken their orders—two lobster roll specials.

He shrugged. "Mostly, yeah. I left for a few years, college and whatnot, but decided I'd seen enough of the outside world and came back home. I've been here ever since. What about you? You said you were from Boston, right?"

"Yep." She was pleased he'd remembered. "Though I went out of state for a few years, too." First for college, then for FBI training at Quantico, then to Richmond, then on to Philly. She'd actually not been back to Boston except to visit for almost ten years, but she left that part out for now.

"So why come here?" he asked.

That was a tougher question. Fortunately, their food showed up, giving her a few seconds to come up with an answer. She leaned back to let the waiter set the plastic baskets before them and snatched a chip. It crunched as she took a moment to think.

In the end, she decided to stick to the truth. "We needed a change, my mom and I," she admitted, eyes hungrily fixed on the almost-overflowing lobster rolls before her. "She found some sites boasting about how beautiful Maine was and started Googling. We saw an article about the artists' colony out here, looked at the pictures, and fell in love." She shrugged. "And here we are."

"It really is beautiful here," Dylan assured her, already hoisting the first of his lobster rolls toward his mouth. "I don't know if you've had a chance to walk the beaches much yet or to wander through the forests, but they're amazing. Just standing on the shore at night, listening to the waves and watching them lap up against the land—I missed it. That's why I had to come home again."

Cookie watched him as he took a big bite, chewing enthusiastically and unabashedly. She did the same, not bothering to try being ladylike. Ladylike had never really been her thing, and she let out a small moan of pleasure as she reveled in the explosion of salty-sweet lobster held together by a scant amount of mayonnaise.

But the lobster wasn't the only thing that held her attention. Dylan was the type of man who was so hot, women overheated just looking at him. And flirting with him the other day had proven that he was also fun to talk with. But his phone call this morning, and now their conversation here, were revealing a deeper, quieter side.

A side that she found incredibly attractive.

"Penny for your thoughts?" he said, grinning when she started a bit. "You looked like you were somewhere else for a second there." Somehow he'd already made his first roll vanish and was halfway through his second.

Cookie managed an apologetic smile. "Sorry. I was just thinking, you remind me of those old stories of philosopher-kings and wise old woodsmen. You know, the guys who were all rugged and active and knew how to do all kinds of things with their hands, but then they'd talk and you'd realize they had all these deep thoughts on top of that." She blushed again, aware she was gushing a bit, but unwilling to lie or hide her interest.

He laughed. "I don't know that I've ever been called a philosopher-king before," he replied after a second. "But thank you." His blue eyes were warm and alive, and Cookie had to exert all her control not to get lost in them.

"So," she asked, changing the subject to save herself further embarrassment, "Did you always want to be a, what, fix-it man? General handyman? All-purpose repairman?"

"No," he replied, his grin vanishing as though it had been whisked away by a magician, leaving a grim, almost solemn expression in its wake. "Actually, growing up there was only one thing I really wanted to be." He leaned in a little, lowering his voice, and Cookie automatically leaned closer as well, until they were only inches apart. Then he shifted so that his lips were dangerously close to her ear and whispered, "A pirate."

She couldn't help it—she squawked with surprised

laughter. Dylan laughed as well. A few of the restaurant's other patrons glanced at them, startled by the sudden noise, and that just made Dylan laugh harder.

"You're terrible." Cookie snorted, slapping his shoulder lightly as she fell back against her chair, still almost hiccupping from laughing so hard. "You totally had me going."

"It's true!" he insisted, still chuckling. "That's what I wanted to be. Pirate Dylan, scourge of the Atlantic. Or at least New England."

Cookie shook her head, grabbing her water and taking a big gulp to help settle her down. Then she studied him, tilting her head to one side and narrowing her eyes. "I'm trying to picture you with gold hoop earrings, an eyepatch, and a bandana around your head. I've gotta say, you could pull it off." What she really meant was, *You'd be dead sexy as a pirate. But you'd probably be dead sexy as an astronaut or a CDC worker too, so that's not saying much.*

Dylan dipped his head at the compliment and started to reply, when a subtle hushing that turned to silence made them glance around. Instantly spotting the problem, Cookie groaned.

"Great," she muttered. "Just great." Because everyone's gaze centered on the man who had just entered the Salty Dog. A tall, dark, bald man wearing an equally dark suit and mirrored sunglasses.

Hunter.

6.

"**I**'LL BE RIGHT back," Cookie assured Dylan, already rising from her seat. She made her way into the restaurant proper just in time to catch Hunter flashing his badge at Larry. The older man had just approached from the kitchen and was still wiping his hands on a dish towel slung over his shoulder.

"Agent O'Neil, FBI," she heard Hunter announce, loud enough for his voice to carry through the whole place. "I need to ask you some questions about Chip Winslow."

"Yeah?" Larry shot back. "What's that scum-sucking leech up to now? Trying to get you to do his dirty work for him?" Though an inch or two shorter than Hunter, Larry Harris had the edge on Cookie's ex-partner in terms of weight and probably muscle as well. The man was built like a fireplug, stocky and solid, with a broad chest, broader shoulders, and great big thick arms. His hair had probably been dark when he was younger, but now it was shot with gray and white, as was the thick beard he kept neatly trimmed. Cookie had heard more than one local claim the Salty Dog was named for its owner's salt-and-pepper appearance as much as his manner.

Hunter wasn't fazed by the restaurant owner's obvious belligerence. "What he's up to is a shelf in the local morgue," he replied, his own tone cold and crisp. "He washed up dead the day before yesterday."

That threw Larry for a loop, Cookie saw, as his eyes widened and his jaw worked before finding his words. "Wait, dead?" he said, his face going slack for a second. "Damn. I hated the little snit, not gonna lie, but that doesn't mean I wanted him dead; just well away from here."

"Be that as it may, I need to know where you were Sunday night and Monday morning." Hunter's tone hadn't changed, nor had his stance. His feet were planted wide and arms crossed over his chest, the very model of the stern government agent. He barely blinked when Cookie slid between him and Larry, just tilted his head up slightly so he could continue to stare at the restaurant owner over her head.

"We need to talk," Cookie told him, keeping her voice low. When he didn't budge, she poked his chest, and her finger practically rebounded off the rock-hard muscle as she added, "Now," sharp enough that he knew it wasn't an idle request.

She moved past him and stomped over toward the coat closet, which was completely empty right now because of the pleasant weather. After a second, and no doubt a don't-go-anywhere growl to Larry, Hunter joined her.

"What the hell are you doing?" Cookie demanded the minute he was standing next to her. "Larry didn't kill anyone."

"Oh? Were you with him Sunday night and Monday morning?" Hunter's tone changed—was that bitterness she heard? "He hardly seems like your type, but what do I know?"

"Stop it," she warned. "Larry's a good guy. He wouldn't do something like this."

"Ah, so you're just basing this on, what, your female intuition?" He finally removed his shades, and as she'd feared, Cookie saw that his eyes had gone so dark they were almost black. That only happened when he was dead set on something—or when he was furious. "I'm sorry to have to tell you this, Charlie, but the FBI doesn't work that way. We require actual facts. And the suspect just admitted that he hated the victim. That's a fact."

"So what?" Cookie snapped. "Sure, he hated Chip. Chip tried—repeatedly—to buy the Salty Dog from him. But Larry also just said he didn't want the guy dead, and you saw for yourself how surprised he was when you told him." She poked Hunter in the chest again. "That's also a fact."

For a second, neither of them moved, and the temperature in the small closet seemed to ratchet up another ten degrees. Then she saw his stony expression crack just a little. "He did look genuinely surprised," Hunter admitted slowly.

Cookie let out the breath she'd been holding, glad that her ex-partner was finally willing to see reason. "Look, we were a great team, right?" she asked, which earned her a short nod. "And you know why?"

"Because we both looked so good in suits?" he said. Which got a quick laugh out of her and an answering upturn at the lips from him. His eyes were lightening, shading back to their more normal warm brown, which was also a good sign. She was reaching him.

"No, but that probably didn't hurt," she agreed. "We were a great team because you're like a bulldog—you never let go, just kept going after each case until we cracked it. But sometimes you got too latched on, too focused on the bone you were gnawing to see the big picture. I kept you grounded. I made you stop and look around and catch your breath and think things through. You were the persistence, I was the perspective." She poked him again, a little more gently. He grabbed her hand, and she let him hold it as she said, "And right now you need that. I can help you, Hunter. I know this place, these people. I can see things you can't. Let me help you."

He studied her a second then sighed as he let her fingers go. "No one here is supposed to know you're FBI," he reminded her—sadly, she thought. "So you can't officially work this case with me as far as they're concerned." She waited, certain there was more coming.

Sure enough, a second later he continued, "But there's nothing that says I can't bring on a local consultant."

"Great." She slapped him on the arm. "See? It'll be like old times. Except that I'm not wearing a suit."

"Pity, that," he replied. Then he glanced back over to where Larry waited. "Well, partner, should we go back to questioning our suspect?"

"By all means." This time Cookie led the way, and she deliberately threw Larry a warm smile to let him know, that from here on out, the questioning would have a very different flavor. "Sorry about that, Larry," she said as they rejoined him. "Just needed to get a few things sorted out. What can you tell us about Chip?"

Larry considered that with a scowl as if he didn't trust the change in tack before he relaxed. "Rich kid," he answered finally. "Grew up somewhere on the mainland, not really sure where. Wanted to make his mark—that's how he put it one time—show his parents he wasn't just living off them. He planned to do something big and impressive and lucrative in his own right, and he fixed on Secret Seal as the place to do it." He shook his head. "Tried talking me into selling him this place any number of times. Tried wheedling, threatening, and throwing huge stacks of money at me. I always said no. It was driving him nuts." Larry chuckled a little at the memory then sobered. "The guy was a jerk, but I'm sorry he's dead."

He turned his attention to Hunter and glowered. "And in answer to your question, Agent O'Neil, I was here Sunday 'til an hour or two after closing then home with my family. Monday morning I stopped by the wharf, like I always do, to pick up the day's catch, then came here in time to get set up before we opened for breakfast." He glanced around the restaurant, and people averted their gazes as if they weren't watching. "Plenty of people saw me each time."

Hunter's only answer to that was a crisp nod. "Anything else you can tell us about Mr. Winslow?" he asked instead. "Was he a frequent customer here?"

That got a bark of laughter from Larry. "Here? No. He knew what I thought of him, so he only came around when he was trying to buy the place off me." He scratched at his beard. "I think he was at the Tipsy Seagull a lot, though."

Cookie responded to Hunter's unspoken question. "It's a local bar right off the docks," she explained. "Not exactly a tourist destination. Most of the regulars are locals, I think."

"Seems like an odd choice for someone like him," Hunter remarked. "But we'll check it out. Thank you, Mr. Harris," he added, returning his attention to Larry and offering a hand. "If I have any more questions, I'll let you know."

"Yeah, sure, fine." Larry shook hands with him, and Cookie was pleased to see that neither of them did the macho thing of trying to outgrip the other. "Hope you catch whoever did this. Even Winslow didn't deserve that."

Hunter paused a second. "What makes you think it wasn't an unfortunate accident?" he asked, though Cookie didn't hear accusation in his tone, just curiosity.

That drew a smile from the restaurant owner. "Rich as he was, I don't think the FBI'd be poking around if it was just an accident, now would you?" he asked. "If you're here and demanding alibis, I'm guessing you think someone did him in." His smile broadened. "And since you're not correcting me, I'm pretty sure that means I'm right."

Hunter actually chuckled at that, acknowledging that he'd been played, and Cookie didn't bother to hide her own grin. She liked Larry—he'd been one of the first to welcome her and Rain when they'd moved here. And though he was gruff to everyone and didn't take crap, she could tell he was a good man beneath the crabby exterior. He was exactly the sort who'd give free food to someone in need but then deny he'd ever done it. The kind who helped, not because he wanted people to see what he'd done or because he thought he should, but because he genuinely cared.

They turned away from Larry—and almost bumped right into Dylan, who had come up behind them at some point during the conversation. "Everything all right here?" he asked Cookie, but his eyes were on Hunter.

Oh great, Cookie thought as she watched her ex-partner automatically puff up. "Everything is fine here, sir," he replied, switching right back into agent-of-ice mode. "And you are?"

"Dylan Creed," Dylan answered, offering a hand. This time she saw Hunter's forearms strain even through his jacket, and answering muscles jumped in Dylan's arm as he responded. Their hands were clamped together like a pair of vices, and both men's brows furrowed from the strain, but neither budged or let out a sound.

Cookie rolled her eyes.

"How well did you know the victim, Mr. Creed?" Hunter asked when the two of them finally let go and stepped back, neither acknowledging defeat, but neither able to claim victory either.

"Who, Chip Winslow?" Dylan shook his head. "I saw him around from time to time. Everybody did. Never really talked to him myself. A guy like that doesn't have much need for a handyman." He said the last bit with a self-deprecating smile, as if he knew that he was so much more than that, and if anyone couldn't figure that out, it was their loss. Though he hadn't glanced her way during that exchange, Cookie felt almost as if that hint had been aimed at her, and she wanted to assure him that she definitely knew he was more. A lot more.

"His loss," Cookie said, a smile tugging at her lips when Dylan glanced her way, giving her a small nod of acknowledgement.

"I see. And where were you Sunday night and Monday morning?" Hunter continued, ignoring her completely. Cookie wanted to scream in frustration or haul off and slug him. What was wrong with him? Dylan wasn't even remotely a suspect.

"Sunday night? I was home," Dylan replied. "Alone. Monday morning I was over at the Secret Seal Inn—maybe you know the place?" That last was thrown out quick and hard, his smile not hiding the edges of the barb, and Cookie caught her breath as she felt Hunter's gaze shift to her, darkening as it moved. Swell.

"Oh?" was all he said, but she knew that tone and knew this was going to be a conversation as soon as they were alone. "I see."

But Cookie hadn't let Hunter push her around when they'd been partners, and she certainly wasn't going to start now. "That's right," she said, keeping her own tone friendly and upbeat. "Dylan's been doing some work on the place for us." She favored him with a smile. "He was already there when I woke up, though Mom could tell you exactly when he got there, I'm sure." There was no way Rain had missed the arrival of a man like Dylan.

She directed a glare at Hunter. "He was with me when Mom found the body. We were up on the porch, and she was back behind the house, down in the water." Meaning, there was no way Dylan could have stashed Chip's body there and made it back around without Rain noticing. Though of course if he'd killed Chip the night before and tossed the body into the water, he wouldn't have had to do anything at all the next morning. But that was ridiculous. She knew in her bones that Dylan had nothing to do with this.

"Got it." She could tell by the edge in Hunter's words that all he'd really heard was 'we were up on the porch,' and her glower at him intensified. Why was he getting so worked up about this? "I'm staying at the inn, as it so happens," Hunter continued, giving Dylan a smile that would have looked at home on a hungry shark. "If you think of anything else."

Dylan just nodded. "I'll let you know if I do," he promised, and if his tone wasn't as frigid as Hunter's, it was equally unyielding, as was his stance. The two were like dogs fighting over their territory. *Better get them apart,* Cookie decided, *before they actually start pissing on each other.* Or her.

"Let's go check out the Tipsy Seagull," Cookie told Hunter, pushing his shoulder until he began to back away. "See what we can find out there." She smiled back at Dylan. "Sorry to have to cut lunch short," she told him, and meant it. "And for other things." She waved a hand in Hunter's direction.

"No problem." Dylan answered her smile, but it wasn't as warm as the ones he'd bestowed upon her earlier. "Maybe some other time."

She didn't look back as she guided Hunter out of the restaurant, but Cookie would have been willing to bet that Dylan watched her until she disappeared out the door.

7.

"**I**DIOT!" COOKIE WAITED only until the door had swung shut behind them before slugging Hunter on the arm as hard as she could. Her knuckles ached from the impact, but she'd be damned if she rubbed them in front of him.

"Hey!" he protested, all traces of the ice-cold agent dropping at once. Instead he looked more like a hurt puppy—albeit one in a nice suit—as he rubbed at his arm. "What was that for?"

"What the hell is wrong with you?" she demanded, walking away and forcing him to jog to catch up. "You can't just go around interrogating everybody you meet."

"Is it 'everybody' you're upset about," he asked as they headed down the seaside road toward the docks, "or just one 'somebody' in particular? Like, say, a certain 'handyman' who couldn't take his eyes off you?"

That defused her anger for just a second. "You think so?" she replied, a slow smile spreading across her face.

"Oh, yeah," Hunter answered. "I practically slipped

in the puddle of drool on the way out."

And then heat rushed through her veins because she was angry again. "So, what, the first guy to show some interest in me, and you treat him like Public Enemy Number One?" She raised her fist again, but this time Hunter was ready and skipped out of range.

"When some guy goes sniffing around my ex-partner like a dog in heat, you're damn right I'm going to step in," he huffed. "Where the hell are we going, anyway?"

"The Tipsy Seagull, I already told you," Cookie snapped back, "and I can take care of myself, thank you very much. I don't need you going all alpha-male on me."

"I'm just trying to look out for you," he argued, but Cookie knew that was only half of it. Oh, sure, Hunter worried about her, she believed that. But he also didn't like Dylan showing interest in her, and that had nothing to do with her being safe and everything to do with him staking a claim. A claim he had no right to, since he hadn't exactly cleared it with her first.

What if he did, though, a part of her wondered. He'd made it clear he was interested last night. That was for sure. But interested in just a quick roll in the hay or in something more? Because as much fun as fooling around with him would be—and she was sure it would be a *lot* of fun—Cookie wasn't actually interested in a one-night stand. Not even with someone as hot as Hunter.

She shoved that whole line of thought from her head as they approached the Tipsy Seagull. It was a ramshackle place, nowhere near as solid or handsome as the Salty Dog. In fact, it looked like a large shack that had been built at the end of the docks and then added to over the years to turn it into a decent-sized bar. Which Cookie suspected was exactly how the place began.

Ducking under the weathered sign bearing a drunk seagull reeling about, Hunter pushed open the door and led the way inside. Cookie followed.

It took a few seconds for her to acclimate to the dim lighting and the sour smell of stale beer and rotting fruit. It was nothing like the Salty Dog, which opened up to the pier in the back. The Tipsy Seagull blocked out any and all sight of the docks or the water beyond. There wasn't even a window. It was as though the patrons here didn't want to even be reminded of the ocean while they drank; which made sense, given that most of them were fishermen, lobstermen, and sailors. They spent all day, every day out there on the water. When they came back to dry land, the last thing they wanted was to think about water again.

Considering its exterior, Cookie had expected the inside to be just as stitched-together and piecemeal, probably with one of those bars that's just a door over a pair of barrels. But the interior, though a bit dark and not at all fancy, was a lot more decent—and more solid—than she'd expected. The bar, in particular, took up the entire side wall and was constructed from dark wood whose grain still showed through years of polish and spilled drinks. Bar stools crowded alongside it, and tables and chairs sat in clusters around the rest of the room.

There weren't all that many people here since it was still midday, but the handful that were sat at the bar, nursing mugs and bottles and the occasional shot glass. Cookie thought a few of them looked vaguely familiar, but she didn't know any of their names.

"Friendly sort of place," Hunter commented, sizing it up before striding over to the bar and claiming an empty stool by the far end. Cookie joined him.

"What can I get you?" the bartender asked. Unlike most of his customers, he wasn't old and grizzled. In fact, Cookie would have put him in his late twenties at most. Tall and thin, with pale skin and long, straight black hair, his features were too pretty to be handsome and not pretty enough to be beautiful, leaving him looking delicate and a little unwell. *He'd look more at home in a Goth band than a dockside bar,* Cookie thought, noting the heavy-metal T-shirt under his plaid flannel and the heavy chain connecting his wallet to his belt.

"Two beers, whatever you've got on tap that's good," Hunter instructed, and Cookie stifled a momentary irritation that he'd ordered for her. He knew her well enough to know she drank beer, and if they were staking things out a little before asking questions, which it seemed they were, beer was a safe choice. They could nurse one for a while without looking too suspicious and without getting fuzzyheaded. Back when they'd worked together, she'd have let him order for her without a problem. It was just now, following on the heels of his run-in with Dylan, that it irked her.

"Hey, remember the Rodriguez case?" Hunter asked her as they settled into their seats. He was grinning, and Cookie found herself smiling as well at the memory.

"How could I forget it?" she asked. "Best excuse for weight gain ever!" Sam Rodriguez had been wanted in connection with a drug cartel, mainly in the hope that he'd flip on his bosses to save his own skin. The only problem was, he'd realized the FBI was on to him and had disappeared. It was as if he were a ghost—there one day, completely gone the next, vanished without a trace. They had absolutely no leads, no ideas, not even any hunches. Nothing.

Until one of Rodriguez's buddies had mentioned going to this bar with him, this old Irish pub. "He always swore it had the best fish and chips in the city," this other guy had claimed. "Used to go there at least once a week, been doing it for years."

So, naturally, the Feds staked out the pub.

But it was a lot easier—and a lot less conspicuous—to stake out the place from inside. They'd divided up the days, and each two-man team had taken its turn as customers at Danny Boy's.

For two whole weeks.

"The fish and chips really were amazing," Cookie recalled with a sigh. "But after scarfing them basically every other day, I couldn't even look at fish and chips for two months. And it was another two months after before

I could order them."

They both laughed, and Cookie found herself relaxing a bit. This was the easy camaraderie she remembered them having.

Just then, the bartender brought over their pints. "Thanks," Hunter said, accepting his and taking a good long sip. "Ah, perfect."

Cookie gulped at hers as well and tried not to notice the metallic flavor of cheap beer. "Nice place," she said, glancing around. "Though… well, never mind."

"What's that, sweetheart?" the bartender asked.

"Oh, it's just"—she paused for effect—"I can't see Chip Winslow coming *in* here."

She'd been watching the bartender closely when she said that, and she saw him wince then scowl. No love lost there.

"Chip Winslow? Please!" the bartender scoffed. "That guy's a total douche. I'd refuse to serve him, but his money's good, so I grit my teeth and bear it."

"Oh?" Hunter interjected. "In that case, it might interest you to hear that Chip Winslow's body washed up on the shore Monday morning."

"What? Hold on, you're saying he's dead?" The bartender stepped back a pace, and the bottles behind him rattled when he bumped into the shelf. "What happened?"

"We were hoping you could tell us," Hunter said. "When was the last time you saw Mr. Winslow?"

The bartender frowned. "Friday, I think," he finally

answered. "Yeah, Friday. He was in here, like usual." He caught Cookie's look of surprise and laughed. "Oh, I know, we ain't exactly fancy, but he was in all the time anyway."

"And you didn't like it?" Cookie prompted. "Or him?"

"I couldn't stand him," the bartender admitted. "Talk about an entitled little prick! I think at least half the reason he drank here was because it made him feel all big and important. Jerk."

Hunter had been sitting quietly, content to let Cookie ask the questions and field the answers, but now he spoke up again. "If that was half the reason," he asked, "what was the other half?"

The bartender shrugged. "Who knows? Dude was a total ass. Maybe he just liked slumming it."

"What was he doing Friday when you saw him?" Cookie asked. She caught his wince. "Please," she asked gently. "We're just trying to figure out what happened to him."

"I threw him out," the bartender finally admitted. "It was either that or let them duke it out right here at the bar. And while he might've deserved that, I'd probably have lost my job for not keeping a handle on things. And I need this job."

"Who was he fighting with?" Cookie asked, leaning forward. She caught the bartender's eyes flicking to her shirt where it fell open, but didn't say anything or change position. Sexuality was a tool like any other, and she had no problem using it. Up to a point.

"Rand," the bartender answered after a few seconds, tearing his gaze away from her chest and shifting it up to her face. "It was him and Rand."

"Who is this Rand?" Hunter asked.

The bartender sighed. "Rand Lambert. He's my sister Mindy's boyfriend." Now that he'd started talking, he seemed unable to stop. "Winslow was hitting on her, and not for the first time. Rand got pissed and got up in the dude's face. Winslow didn't back down, which means he was either crazy, stupid, plastered, or suicidal, and I had to stop them from actually getting into it right here. Fortunately Mindy helped talk Rand down, and they left. Winslow kept going on about it, though, so eventually I got fed up and told him to get the hell out."

Cookie and Hunter exchanged a glance. Hunter got the question out first. "Where can we find Rand Lambert?"

"He works at Kelly's. He's there most of the time," the bartender replied.

"It's the local gym," Cookie explained to Hunter. "It's only a few blocks from here." She turned back to the bartender. "Thanks."

He shrugged. "You really think Rand killed him or something?" She could tell that his concern over ratting out his friend was warring with his desire for gossip.

"We're just exploring every lead," she answered, downing the rest of her beer in a single long gulp as she hopped off the stool. "We appreciate all your help."

Cookie led the way back out onto the street. The sunshine was welcome, and a seagull called out overhead as if he agreed. "Kelly's is this way," she told Hunter, who had followed her out.

"Sounds like Winslow was really good at making enemies," her ex-partner commented as he caught up to her.

"Definitely," Cookie agreed. "But we still don't know how he died. It could have been an accident."

"Could've been," he admitted. "Or maybe somebody else helped it along." He shrugged. "Just exploring all the options for now. Let's talk to this Rand guy and see how he fits."

Cookie couldn't argue with that, so she kept her mouth shut as she led the way up the sloping hill toward the gym. Still, she had to admit that it was nice working with Hunter again, even if only for a little while. His whole macho I'm-the-*man* act aside, he was a good guy, and they'd always clicked.

The question remained, was that clicking work-only, or did it extend outside the job? It was something she'd wondered about plenty of times back in Philly, and once she and Rain had fled, she'd assumed she'd never know the answer.

Now she thought she just might find out after all.

8.

"OKAY, NOT QUITE what I was expecting," Hunter admitted as they slowed to a stop outside Kelly's.

Cookie had to laugh at his tone, and his expression. "It's no Crunch or Gold's or any of those," she said. "Out here, you want to work out, you go to Kelly's. Or you exercise at home."

She hadn't cared much one way or the other, but then she'd always preferred to practice her yoga, tai chi, and stomach crunches in the privacy of her own home. She knew that Hunter was a nut for staying in shape and working out. And even though she'd never seen the inside of his apartment—that had been a very definite line she hadn't been prepared to cross—she'd always assumed it would be all chrome and marble and steel, sharp edges and bright surfaces. Which made her think that Hunter probably preferred for his gym to be the same way; modern, slick, and high-tech.

Kelly's was none of those things.

It looked as if it had been there a hundred years, with its weathered stone exterior and the painted sign over the door that probably needed to be touched up every summer. And when they stepped inside, she saw that the interior was exactly the same. A single open room took up most of the space, with a twenty-foot ceiling pierced by skylights for added light. A boxing ring dominated one side of the room, with heavy bags and punching bags all around it. The other side was weight machines and free weights. She did see one rowing machine but guessed its presence on the isolated island was meant to be ironic. A door past all the equipment presumably led to lockers and showers, and she assumed that was where the odor that reminded her of a dead animal must be coming from. A wrought-iron staircase in one corner spiraled up to a glass-fronted office.

All in all, the place looked as if it hadn't been updated since before the days of saddle shoes and poodle skirts.

It was mostly empty, with two guys using one of the heavy bags, the staccato sound of fists punching the leather echoing through the quiet space, while one lone guy was lifting free weights, one weight for each hand. When he spotted Cookie and Hunter, he set the weights down and sauntered on over. He was a typical gym rat, so built up he couldn't lower his arms all the way to his side. His neck thickened into a collar of muscle, and a snug white sleeveless tee showed off all that dedication.

"What do you guys need?" he asked as he closed the

distance to them. His dark-brown hair had been buzzed short and suited his thick—some would say rugged—features. He wasn't a bad-looking guy, Cookie thought. If you were into that sort.

"FBI," Hunter announced, flashing his badge. A part of Cookie couldn't help but wonder if that little display had been as much for her benefit as for the gym rat—showing her what she had given up when she'd left.

As if she didn't remember all the bloody time.

"We're looking for Rand Lambert," Hunter declared.

Cookie wasn't even a little bit surprised when the gym rat ground to a halt just shy of them. "I'm Rand," he acknowledged, the muscles in his upper arms, chest, and shoulders flexing as if he was about to make a break for it. But Hunter's right hand slid under his suit jacket, and Rand froze.

"We wanted to ask you a few questions about you and Chip Winslow," Cookie explained. "We hear the two of you got into it a few nights ago, over at the Tipsy Seagull."

"That's right," Rand admitted. "He was hitting on my girl. I told him to knock it off before I knocked him *out*, but he wouldn't listen. Ian, Mindy's brother, stopped me from rearranging Chip's face. Mindy and I left. That's it."

Cookie frowned as she considered the big, beefy guy in front of her. He didn't look very happy, but to her eye he wasn't acting all that guilty, either. Less like a man trying to hide his involvement in a murder and more like a man unwilling to admit he had a temper. She caught Hunter's eye and shook her head, just barely. He sighed, but some of the tension fled his stance.

"Anybody else see what happened?" Cookie asked.

Rand nodded. "Sure, everybody else at the Tipsy Seagull." He tossed off a few names. "Ask them. They'll vouch for me." Then he frowned. "Why're you asking about Winslow? He finally get what was coming to him?"

"He did," Cookie confirmed. "Any idea who else besides you might want to help him get there?"

"You need to talk to Larry Harris," Rand replied without a second's hesitation. "Dude hates Winslow even more than I do." He frowned, dark-brown eyes focusing on something well past her. "Heck, I'd look at the whole family, if I was you. Larry's kids, Daisy and Stone, they don't like Winslow either. And Stone's got a record."

"Stone?" Hunter asked.

Cookie sighed. "Stone Harris. I've seen him around enough to know who he is. He's a total stoner. When he's not at the Salty Dog, he's wandering around town or sunning himself out by the beach on the hood of his old Subaru." She gave Rand a sharp look. "I'd be willing to bet his only 'record' is multiple counts of possession, sprinkled with a few possessions with intent and maybe a DUI or two for good measure."

"Hey, a crime's a crime, right?" Rand shrugged. "You wanted to know who'd be happy to take Winslow down, it's them."

"Just because others hated the guy too doesn't make you any less of a suspect," Hunter pointed out, staring Rand down until the big gym rat faltered and turned away. "Where'd you go after Mindy dragged you out of there that night?"

The scowl on Rand's face slowly transformed itself into a broad, leering grin. "Back to my place," he answered slowly, all but licking his lips. "I had a lot of aggression to… work off."

Cookie could feel herself flushing under his suggestive gaze. And she had absolutely no question that he was telling the truth. "Thank you," she managed to sputter out through suddenly dry lips. "If we have any other questions, we'll let you know."

He nodded and turned around, heading back to the free weights. Cookie watched him go. If you liked them big and beefy, Rand Lambert was certainly one very impressive specimen.

Evidently, Hunter was less impressed. "I'm liking him for this," he insisted as he and Cookie stepped back out of the gym a few minutes later. "He's got motive, clearly, and just look at the guy—he's a poster child for steroid use. He probably waited around the Tipsy Seagull for Winslow to leave and then beat him to death with those oversized Popeye arms of his. Mindy'll cover for him, of course—they probably did go back to his place and keep busy all night, things just got started a little later than he claimed."

Cookie could see the logic there, linking every detail

together. Rand did make an almost ideal suspect.

The only problem was, she didn't believe it.

And Hunter could tell that by looking at her. "You're not buying it," he noted as they retraced their steps through a quaint residential section of town in the direction of the inn. "Why not?"

"I don't know," she admitted, shaking her head and sending her long hair cascading about her. "I'm just not. It all makes sense, and you could probably convince a jury, especially if Rand has a history of violent behavior. I just don't think he did it."

Neither of them said anything for another minute. Then Hunter laughed. "I've missed this," he told her. "The arguing back and forth over witnesses, suspects, alibis, motives, and all the rest." He favored her with a small, almost-shy smile that warmed her insides. This was the sweet, thoughtful Hunter that lived hidden beneath the other's overpowering machismo and only let her catch glimpses of him through the cracks. "I always liked the way you never let me get away with sloppy policework," he told her. "You made me earn each and every case."

Cookie shrugged and fought to keep the grin off her face. "No point if you didn't have to work for it," she reminded him, citing an old saying she'd appropriated after seeing it on a poster. That was how she'd built her career, never settling for the easy win. On anything.

Which had been yet another reason for not sleeping with Hunter. He'd made it very easy for her to say yes, but she'd always known that if she had, she'd have wound up regretting it. Because sleeping with him would have been incredibly simple—and the next day she'd have discovered he'd already moved on and set his sights on some other equally-easy target.

No, she'd decided right after being partnered with him years ago. She wasn't going to make it that effortless for him. If he really was interested, he'd have to work for it.

She did, however, throw him a bone. "I've missed working with you, too," she replied and almost laughed at the bright, boyish smile that creased his face. What stopped her was the mental reminder that Hunter was only up here because she'd asked him to look into this case. Once it was over, he'd be gone again. And while Cookie could hardly blame him for fleeing back to civilization, it also meant he'd be making a choice—her or Philly.

And she wasn't willing to let him claim both of them, only to leave her behind afterward. She was worth more than that, and they both knew it.

9.

"OKAY," COOKIE ASKED, "what now? The girlfriend?"

"The girlfriend," Hunter agreed. "Mindy. You know her?"

Cookie shook her head. "We've only been here a few weeks," she reminded him. "I've met a few people, like Larry, and seen plenty of others, but she's not one of them." She sighed. "I'm not even sure where to find her." She pulled out her phone. "But I think I know someone who would."

"We can't go involving any potential suspects or giving them a heads-up about our investigation," Hunter said. Her sudden flash of irritation at him for reminding her of basic procedure as if she were a wet-behind-the-ears rookie again vanished when she realized he'd just referred to it as "our" investigation.

"Trust me," she replied as her fingernail tapped on the phone, "I didn't forget. The person I'm calling isn't even remotely a suspect, but I'd be willing to bet she could name every person on this island and tell you where they live, where they work, what they like to eat, their favorite drink, and probably a half dozen other facts." She dialed and lifted the phone to her ear. "Mom? Listen, I need to know about a local girl named Mindy…"

A few seconds, later she ended the call and grinned at her ex-partner. "Mindy Tremaine," she reported smugly. "Too pretty for her own good, and knows it, according to Rain. More importantly, she makes her living as a hair stylist and owns the salon down the street."

Hunter shook his head, laughing. "What, no favorite color?" he said. "Tell your mom I'm disappointed. She's going to have to work at it a bit more if she wants to earn favorite CI status."

They were both smiling as they turned around and headed back toward the heart of town, and Cookie savored the moment. This was what it had been like between them at its best, both of them intent on catching the bad guys, both of them knowing the other had their back, trusting each other's instincts and dedication. This was what she missed.

"So is everything on this one street?" Hunter asked a few minutes later, his tone light and teasing as they passed the gym and a handful of other mom-and-pop businesses. "There aren't any other streets, are there? Makes it easy to find things, I guess."

"What do you want?" Cookie answered. "It's an island. There's maybe four hundred people here, tops, though that's doubled in summer, they tell me. That's when the artists' colony comes out."

"An artists' colony?" She could hear the derision dripping from his words. "Oh, joy. A bunch of 'artistes' wandering around telling everyone their run-down old eyesores 'sing with authenticity' and 'speak to the soul of perseverance' and 'glisten with the promise of a rainbow's inner vision.'"

"Wow, you're pretty good at artist-speak," Cookie accused, a wicked smile touching her lips. "You sure you aren't hiding something from me? You go home and splash paint around on a canvas and then stare at it, weeping at the beauty of the patterns?"

That earned a snort from him. "Yeah, right." Then he brightened, his grin just as mischievous as her own. "Hey, are you sure it's just an artist colony? Not, say, a nudist colony? The two go hand in hand, right?" He started laughing. "I can picture it now, you and your mom awash in old, wrinkled, naked people who just want to stand around and talk about art and color while their junk's in your face."

"Shut up." Cookie swatted at him, trying to drive out the image he'd just inserted in her head. Then the vision of Rain mingling with their unclothed guests, just as naked as they were and just as uncaring, sent a horrifying shudder through her. She needed brain bleach.

They were still laughing as they strolled up to Mindy's workplace, whose small sign made Cookie laugh harder while it took Hunter longer to get the joke. It read Clip, Dip & Rip.

He said, "Wait. Does that…?"

Cookie nodded. She had to hand it to Mindy—it was a memorable name. "After you," she said, pulling the door open for Hunter.

The salon wasn't terribly big, she saw as she followed Hunter inside. There were several reclining chairs, each one set in front of a sink with a mirror mounted on the wall behind it. A row of chairs along the opposite wall were outfitted with old-fashioned hair dryers hung over each seat. It again felt as if she'd stepped into the fifties, complete with the ammonia odor of perm solution, and she glanced down at herself, half-expecting to see that she was now wearing a poodle skirt.

There weren't any customers in the salon at the moment, and a woman sat in one of the chairs, thumbing through an old fashion magazine. She glanced up and smiled as Cookie and Hunter entered. "Hi, welcome to the Clip, Dip and Rip," she chirped with a straight face. "What do you need today? Haircut?" She eyed Cookie's long, thick hair, which was windswept from all the walking, before turning to study Hunter. "Shave?" Her eyes darted down and back up his body as if she hoped he hadn't noticed. "Wax?"

Hunter cleared his throat, and Cookie smirked at his pink-tinged ears as he replied, "You must be Mindy." Her resemblance to her brother was obvious, but whereas Ian's delicate features made him look frail, they gave Mindy an ethereal beauty. Combined with her long, glossy black hair, she looked like a fashion model.

"That's right," she answered, rising from the chair and stepping across to them. She even moved like a model, gliding as if she were floating on air. That was a trick Cookie herself had certainly never mastered. A fact Rain reminded her of often enough by shrieking that the ceiling was coming down on her head whenever Cookie thundered down the stairs. "Did someone recommend me?"

"Something like that," Cookie agreed, nodding to Hunter, who flashed his badge. "We need to ask you some questions about Chip Winslow."

Mindy instantly dropped the sales pitch, her bright smile collapsing into a sullen pout that made her look like a rich but spoiled teen princess. "Crap, what did Rand do now?" she asked, retreating to her chair and flopping down into it. Cookie stared at her, mouth parted, amazed at the way the girl landed in a pose more suited for a renaissance painting than the Clip, Dip & Rip. Even when flailing, the girl was still more graceful than she could've ever managed. Not that she was jealous or anything. "I told him to just leave it alone. Chip didn't mean anything by it. He was just being friendly."

"Friendly?" Hunter pounced on the word like a hawk. "Way we heard it, he was all over you at the Tipsy Seagull. Rand got in his face about it, and Winslow refused to back off. You and your brother had to pull them apart before your boyfriend tore the poor guy's head off."

Mindy laughed, and it was a sharp, cutting sound. "Poor guy? Don't let Chip hear you call him that. He'd go nuts! Poor is about the last thing he wants to be." She shrugged, her straight, silky hair floating about her shoulders. "Yeah, so Chip was hitting on me. So what? It's not like I haven't flirted with him plenty. He's a regular, comes in whenever he's on the island to get his hair cut and his nails done." She smirked. "And he tips well. Really well."

Hunter cleared his throat. "That must not have made Rand very happy."

"Maybe not, but he understood. Girl's gotta earn a living, right?" She eyed the two of them suspiciously. "What's this all about? That tussle at the Seagull? Or is something else going on?"

"Where were you the rest of that night?" Hunter asked, not bothering to answer her question.

"With Rand," Mindy answered. She flushed, but at the same time her smirk widened. "We were... busy. All night."

Yet another image Cookie didn't need seared in her brain. She frowned. "You know anybody else who had a beef with Chip Winslow? Anybody who'd want to hurt him?"

Mindy didn't even have to think about that one. "Have you talked to Daisy Harris yet?" she asked, scowling. "She had a thing for Chip, but he wouldn't give her the time of day. Said she was 'too common' for him. That pissed her off something fierce." She flicked her hair back over her shoulder. "Daisy's used to getting what she wants. Girl's got a serious temper, too. Spoiled and vicious, not a good combination." She smiled, a slow, nasty smile. "Somebody put a hurt on Chip, my money's on Daisy."

Cookie glanced over at Hunter, who met her gaze. She could tell he was thinking the same thing she was. That was twice Daisy's name had come up, and everybody on the island knew about Chip's disagreements with Larry. At the same time, the two people pointing the finger at this girl were Mindy and her boyfriend, who even if they hadn't rehearsed their stories would have similar attitudes and probably shared gripes. So it wasn't conclusive or anything, but obviously they would want to talk to Daisy, even if just to rule her out.

"Thank you for your time," Hunter told Mindy, his tone polite, sympathetic, but a little distant. Which was good, since she was eyeing him up and down, clearly evaluating his looks, his physique, and the quality of his clothes.

Looking to trade up, Cookie thought. She was willing to admit to the needles of jealousy and possessiveness spiking through her now. Sure, she'd turned down Hunter's suggestion last night, and they were only ex-partners, but she still had some claim on him. And she'd be damned if she'd see him get scooped up by an obvious gold-digger like Mindy Tremaine.

Hunter was nobody's fool, though, and he was a playah, he didn't get played. "If you think of anything else, please let me know," he continued, offering Mindy his card.

"Oh, I definitely will," she all but purred back, wrapping her fingers around his as she took the card. "Thank you so much for stopping by." She threw Cookie only the briefest of looks, a dismissive glance that clearly said, 'Don't even bother, girlfriend, he's all mine.' It was all Cookie could manage not to laugh in the other girl's face—right before flattening it with a right hook.

"Well, she's a piece of work," Cookie said as soon as the salon's door had swung shut behind them.

"What, you're not going to be getting your nails done there and gossiping about all the other girls?" Hunter asked, his face showing fake shock. "But you could be besties."

"Yeah, right." Cookie shook her head. "I remember girls like her from school. They ruled the roost and made life miserable for anybody who didn't follow their lead— or for anyone who they thought was a threat."

"Like you?" Hunter asked.

Cookie laughed, though even to her ears it sounded a little bitter. "Me? Not likely. I was a wallflower in school, kept to myself, had my nose in a book. I'd have been completely beneath her notice." She sighed. "Part of me wants to discount Daisy as a suspect just because Mindy so clearly has it out for her, and anybody that girl dislikes so much can't be all bad."

"But you won't, because you're too good to let emo- tions—yours or anybody else's—color the investigation,"

Hunter finished for her. He glanced up at the sky, gauging the sun and the clouds, then looked at his watch. "Listen, we've been at this for a while, and I don't know about you, but all this walking around and fresh air is starting to take a toll. Why don't we head back to the inn, maybe grab a bite, talk over what we've found so far, and figure out what to do next? One good thing about this being an island is that our suspects aren't likely to go anywhere any time soon."

"Works for me," Cookie agreed. It got dark quickly out here, and the idea of putting her feet up and sipping something cold sounded good right about now. She could probably eat, too. Lunch felt as if it had been ages ago.

As she led the way back to the inn, though, she wondered just how much they really had to talk about. It felt as if they had a whole bunch of suspects and absolutely no leads. The case was going nowhere fast. They'd have to up their game before the investigation was declared dead and buried in Deputy Swan's filing cabinet.

10.

BACK AT THE inn, all seemed quiet.

Too quiet.

"Mom?" Cookie called up the stairs. "Hello?"

Rain had already disappeared more than a few times in the short while they'd been on the island. She'd just go out for a walk, leaving behind her keys, phone, ID, money, and often shoes, and reappear three or four hours later, completely unapologetic about how much time had passed. Cookie, meanwhile, would be completely frantic and on the verge of mounting an armed patrol to seek out her mother and punish the dastardly villains who had clearly kidnapped her, because otherwise she certainly would have returned by now. Or at the very least called to say she was still alive.

"Out here, sweetie," her mother answered, the call coming through the kitchen.

Cookie breathed a sigh of relief and headed toward the back door, Hunter in tow, to find her mother. But she wasn't alone.

"It was terrible," Rain was saying. "I nearly died! So I figure I deserve a little something to calm my nerves, don't you? It's only fair."

"More than fair," their guest, Mary Seiger, replied.

"Mom!" Cookie gasped, stopping in the doorway and trying in vain to block Hunter's view or exit. "What are you doing?"

"What does it look like I'm doing?" Rain replied, reclining in her hammock. There were several out back in addition to the two hanging along the front porch, making it very clear that life here on the island was easy, laid-back, and didn't require a whole lot of effort. She was dressed at least, which Cookie was thankful for, wearing her customary short-shorts and tie-dyed tank top, and she had on enormous sunglasses that blocked not only her eyes, but also half her face.

Unfortunately, they did nothing to hide the joint currently dangling from her lips.

"Care for a hit, dear?" Rain asked, offering the joint to her. The skunky smell wafted toward Cookie, making her think she might just get a contact high. "Good stuff, this. Got it from the local boy, the one with the amusingly apt name. Amazed he can get something this fine out here, but I'm certainly not one to look a gift horse in the mouth."

"No, I don't want any!" Cookie hissed, trying to keep her voice down even though she knew it wouldn't help much. Hunter right behind her, after all, so close she could feel the heat radiating off his body.

Which normally would be all kinds of distracting, but right now she was a little too focused on her pot-smoking mother and the woman lounging in the hammock beside her.

"Your loss," Mary commented, reaching out lazily and accepting the joint from Rain. "Your mother's right, this is some really good pot right here."

Hunter poked Cookie in the side right then, and her involuntary jump gave him just enough space to squeeze past her and finally step outside. "Hello again, Ms. James," he said politely. "Mrs. Seiger, we met this morning. How are you ladies this fine day?" Cookie noticed that his eyes were very carefully staying on the women's gazes rather than the contraband in their hands or mouths.

"Oh, couldn't be better," Rain replied with a breezy laugh. "Especially now that you're here. I hope Cookie's been showing you the sights?" *Her meaning couldn't have been clearer if it had been painted on the side of a barn,* Cookie thought as her face flamed with embarrassment.

"We've been having a very enlightening day," Hunter answered with surprising diplomacy. He glanced back over his shoulder and winked at her. "I don't know that I've seen as much as I'd like yet, but I'm hoping it's just a matter of time."

"You smooth-talker, you!" Rain exclaimed, all but slapping her side as she laughed so hard she almost fell out of the hammock. "Handsome and glib! Tell you what, if my daughter's so foolish as to pass, you come see me, hmm? I'd be happy to show you all the sights myself." Rain ran her suggestive gaze down his body, and Cookie couldn't decide if she should laugh or gag.

She was distracted from having to make a choice, however, as a new figure came barreling around the side of the house.

"There you are, Mary!" Henry exclaimed. "I've been looking everywhere. I thought we were going to take a stroll along the beach before we—" He stopped midsentence, staring in shock as his wife of thirty years puffed on the joint before relinquishing it to Rain. He frowned and then sputtered as his face turned the shade of a tomato. "What are you doing?"

"I'm getting high, dear. What does it look like?" Mary said this as if it were the most obvious thing in the world—which, to be fair, it really was. "Would you care for a hit?"

"No, I don't want a hit!" Henry snarled, stomping over to her hammock. "And neither do you. What is wrong with you?" He glared at her then switched his ire to Rain. "This is all your fault!" he accused. "We came here for a nice, relaxing getaway—not to get stoned with some ancient hippie."

Rain, of course, didn't exactly help matters with her reply. "I'd say she's pretty relaxed right about now."

She had a point.

"Come on, Mary!" Henry reached out and grabbed his wife by the arm, practically hauling her from the hammock. Cookie tensed and saw Hunter do the same, but Mary didn't resist, and her husband wasn't hurting her, which meant they really didn't have any right to interfere. Much as Cookie might want to.

"But there's still at least half the joint left," Mary protested even as she let her husband half-lead and half-drag her away. She glanced longingly at Rain. "Couldn't we at least finish it?"

"Oh, we're finished here all right," her husband declared. He glowered at Rain, who was oblivious, before turning to Cookie instead. "We're cancelling the rest of our reservation. I'm putting Mary in the car and going upstairs to pack our things. Then we're gone."

"Please, Mr. Seiger," Cookie pleaded. "Don't go. I'm sorry about… all this, but I'm sure we can fix it. We'd really like you to stay. How about a nice dinner on us? Rain—uh… I make a mean lobster thermidor."

She thought he was softening a little, and reached out toward him, but just then Rain giggled behind her. And, as Cookie watched, Henry's face hardened again.

"I'm sorry, Ms. James," he told her as stiffly as an undertaker. "But we simply can't stay here a minute longer." He stepped a little closer to her and lowered his voice, though only a notch, as he continued, "You should really do something about her, you know. She's going to continue to drive away guests if you don't."

Then he swiveled back around and walked away, taking his wife with him. Her voice trailed off as she began to talk about how pretty the flower gardens were.

Cookie just stared after them for a second before she

spun about to stare down at her mother.

"Really, Mom?" she admonished. "Our first real guests, and you drive them away by getting high with one of them? And not just that, but in front of an FBI agent. Hunter could arrest you right now if he wanted to."

Hunter was very carefully studying the darkening sky as if searching for enemy planes, alien saucers, low-flying ducks, or pretty much anything but the scene unfolding right in front of him.

"Oh, he wouldn't do that, would you, sweetie?" Rain asked casually.

"I would if I were to see you smoking an illegal substance such as marijuana," Hunter replied carefully, his eyes still on the sky. "Which I do not."

"See? He's a good one," Rain assured Cookie. "Latch onto him now, sweetie, before he gets away." She laughed and took another hit.

"This isn't funny, Mom!" Cookie insisted. "The Seigers were our guests. Now they're gone. How, exactly, are we going to afford this place if no one wants to come stay here?" Cookie's heart pounded in anger against her chest.

But her mother was unmoved as she took a deep drag of her joint. "You worry too much," she advised in the strained voice of one that is holding their breath before exhaling long and loudly. "It'll make you old before your time, dear. Take a page out of my book. Just relax a bit, go with the flow. You'll live longer."

"I won't live longer, because I'll starve to death as the owner of an inn no one wants to visit!" Cookie shouted, finally losing her temper at her mother's antics. "Which I wouldn't have to worry about if you'd grow up a little. Stop acting like a rebellious teen for one minute!"

Rain threw her head back, and the hammock careened dangerously with her motion, threatening to toss her out. "Ooh, I'd love to be a teen again." She swung back up, looked past Cookie, and winked at Hunter. "You should've seen me then," she said with a slow smile. "I'd have knocked your socks off."

"I can believe that," he answered before once again looking away. Rain just laughed.

"We're going inside," Cookie told her, tired of fighting and realizing she couldn't win this argument anyway. In order to do that, she'd first have to get her mother to listen and acknowledge what she'd done. And that clearly wasn't going to happen considering the state she was in. "We're going to see about finding some dinner. You can stay out here and do whatever you want. That's up to you."

As she turned to head back inside, though, Cookie couldn't resist saying over her shoulder, "Maybe, since you seem to already know everybody on the island, you can make friends with some of the locals, hmm? That way you won't have to sit around scaring off all our guests instead."

Then she stomped off. Hunter wisely chose to follow, but only at a safe distance.

11.

"MORNING."

Cookie's keyboard stopped clicking as she glanced up from the laptop, and felt the smile breaking across her face. "Morning," she replied to Dylan, who'd just wandered back into the living room-slash-office. His tone had been noncommittal, almost businesslike. But when he saw her smile, his own face relaxed and he returned the expression.

His words still came out a little brusque, however, when he asked, "Where's your bodyguard?"

She started to chuckle then sighed, so it came out as a mix of the two. "Off in town conferring with Deputy Swan, I think."

Dylan fingered one of the little trinkets on the desk between them, a classic hula-girl swivel doll Rain used to have mounted on her dash all through Cookie's childhood. "You two together?" he asked, not looking at her.

"Me and Hunter?" That drew a full-on snort from

her. "Not likely. He's a little too... possessive for my tastes."

Truth be told, Hunter had come on to her again last night. After the whole incident with Rain, Cookie had worked out her aggressions in the kitchen, pounding some veal for scaloppini and the like. Hunter had given her some space, offering to help fetch ingredients but otherwise keeping out of her way. They'd had a slightly tense dinner, filled with silence because Cookie was still stewing. Hunter clearly didn't know how to safely breach that anger, but she'd calmed down as they ate and by the end of the meal was feeling almost mellow again. That was when he'd suggested that he could think of a great way to relax, release all her tension, and also work out any remaining aggression in a far more useful manner.

And, for the second night in a row, Cookie had turned him down. It was obvious Hunter hadn't expected that. In fact, he was so unused to rejection he didn't even know how to process it. He'd actually started rising from his seat, grinning, before her refusal had sunk in and he'd frozen mid-motion. It had been almost laughable, seeing her egotistical ex-partner so utterly shocked.

But it hadn't made her change her mind. Oh, sure, sleeping with Hunter would probably be amazing. Cookie recognized that. And it was certainly something she'd dreamed about and lusted for all the years they'd worked together. But now, when it was right here, when he was actually offering that to her? It just didn't feel right. And part of that, she knew, was the distance that had grown between them, both physical and emotional.

But part of it was also the guy standing in front of her right now. A guy she barely knew yet had a definite attraction to. A guy who had made it clear he was attracted to her as well. A guy she was really interested in getting to know better. A guy that would be staying around Secret Seal Isle. And she couldn't very well pursue that line of thought if she was hopping into bed with Hunter; no matter how much certain portions of her might enjoy that.

"Oh." Dylan's single exclamation brought Cookie back the present. He had raised his eyes from the hula girl, and in them she saw warmth, affection, and interest echo in the slow smile once again spreading along his lips. "Well. Good." She almost laughed again but knew that wouldn't sit well with his already slightly-battered ego. The quiet stretched between them a few seconds before he nodded. "I'd better go finish that porch railing."

"That'd be great, thanks." She hoped her warm tone made it clear that she wasn't dismissing him, and he seemed to get the hint. At least, when he turned to walk away, it wasn't in a huff, and he was still smiling as he went.

It was a nice smile, and one that lit a heat deep inside her. Cookie hoped she'd see a lot more of it.

"HOW'S IT GOING?" she asked as she stepped out onto the porch a few hours later. A cool breeze blew off the ocean and made her hair tickle the back of her neck. "It looks great."

"Just about done," Dylan informed her, dabbing a little more paint on one of the rails then touching up another one. He leaned back and squinted. As he had the other day, he'd evidently overheated too much to remain fully clothed and had stripped off his shirt, something Cookie most certainly approved of wholeheartedly. "There. All set."

He carefully placed the brush down on top of the open paint can and rose smoothly to his feet, the wood beneath him creaking as he backed away toward her so that he could survey the entire porch. Cookie did the same. It really did look great. He'd gotten all of the new rails installed and had painted all of them, the fresh coat still glistening in the late-morning sun, and it all looked clean and new and perfect.

"Of course, now the rest of the place looks terrible by comparison," she pointed out with a smile, indicating the worn shutters and shingles of the wall behind her. "Guess I'll have to get you to work on that next."

Dylan grinned at her. "Why, Ms. James, are you inventing reasons to keep me around?" he teased, his accent lending a delightful near-burr to his words.

"Do I need to?" she flirted back, which only made his grin widen. Then she held up one of the glasses in her hand. "I brought you some lemonade. Figured you might get a little dehydrated out here." She let her gaze slide openly across his sweaty chest, shoulders, and arms.

"Thanks, that sounds great." Stepping forward, he took the glass from her, their hands touching for just a second, but it was enough to send a jolt clean through her. She thought by the way his eyes widened that he'd felt it as well.

"Shall we?" she asked to cover her surprise, indicating a pair of the porch chairs nearby. He nodded, and they sat, both balancing their glasses on the broad arms of their chairs.

"I'm really sorry about lunch yesterday," Cookie started after they'd both had a few sips. "I mean, the way it ended. I'm not sorry about the rest."

"Me either," he agreed. "Though, yeah, not the ending I saw in my head."

"Oh? And what did you see?"

His answering smile lit her body up as though she'd touched a live wire.

Wow, if he can do that to me just by smiling, what would it be like if he was more... hands-on?

The thought immediately made her flush, and she toyed with her glass in the hopes of hiding her reaction, but when she glanced up she found him watching her intently, his blue eyes piercing and knowing and just a little bit smug.

"Maybe we should try again," she suggested softly.

"I'd like that," he agreed at once. But then a shadow passed over his face. "Provided your bodyguard isn't around to disrupt it again." He downed a quarter of his drink before continuing. "Is he your ex?"

Cookie considered how to answer that. "In a manner of speaking," she said finally. She sipped on her lemonade, and the sourness made her jaw clench. After all, that was true enough, in its way. She wanted to tell Dylan all about it, why she was really here, who she'd been before, but wasn't sure she was ready to share that with him. Or that it was entirely safe to do so. She wasn't in the witness protection program or anything—she'd moved of her own accord and so wasn't bound by any rules or strictures—but it didn't seem the wisest or safest course to reveal her true identity to someone she'd only recently met, no matter how strong the chemistry between them.

"Did he come up here to win you back?" Dylan asked next, his eyes intent on her.

That was something she could answer easily. "No. At least, I don't think so." She frowned as she realized maybe that had been part of the reason for his prompt response, but shook it off. "I called him," she explained. "After the body turned up."

"Because he's FBI, and you didn't trust Swan to get to the bottom of things." Dylan nodded. "Yeah, I get that. He's not a bad guy, but he's not exactly the most dedicated public servant, either. Pretty sure the reason he drew Secret Seal as his beat is because it was a good way to keep him out of trouble." He took another sip. "And his aunt's the mayor in Hancock, so firing him isn't exactly an option."

"Ah." That certainly explained things better. Cookie made a mental note to tell Hunter, if he hadn't found that out already himself. Talking about all this reminded her of their investigation, and she decided she might as well use this opportunity to get a little more information. "What can you tell me about Daisy Harris?"

"Daisy?" It was like a wall came down inside Dylan. She practically saw the light vanish from his eyes, his sunny blue gaze turning to cold steel in a heartbeat. "What do you want to know?" The playfulness had vanished from his voice as well.

She shrugged, deliberately working to play it casual. "Oh, you know, the usual. What's she like? She works at the Salty Dog, right?"

"She does," Dylan agreed, dragging out each of the two words. "She does the books and sometimes waits tables or manages if they're busy. Larry's handed most of the business side off to her at this point, which leaves him free to cook and greet and inspect the catch." He studied her. "Is she a suspect?" he asked bluntly.

"I don't know. Should she be?" Cookie asked. "Her name's come up a few times, that's all."

Dylan narrowed his eyes at her. "Is there some reason you're doing the investigating and not Mr. FBI? You are, after all, just an innkeeper, right? Or does your ex find me too intimidating?" That last bit was added with a smug smirk.

"I'm just helping him out," Cookie said quickly,

ignoring the jab about being her ex. "Out here he doesn't have a team, and… well, I have some experience with law enforcement. It's only for this case, until he leaves." She held her breath, hoping he wouldn't ask more questions.

"Law enforcement?" There was interest staring back at her.

She met his gaze head-on, preferring to be as straight with him as possible, while still keeping her secrets… for now. "It's not something I'm ready to talk about. Besides, that's the past. If the body hadn't shown up in my backyard, I wouldn't be involved in this at all." Neither would Hunter, but she decided it was best to leave that part out.

He stared at her for a moment then nodded as if he understood where she was coming from. "Okay, fair enough."

"Thanks. Now, about Daisy…?"

"Daisy wouldn't hurt a fly," Dylan assured her. He frowned. "Well, all right, I take that back. She's not a fan of flies. And if you mess with her family, she'll hit you like a freight train. She's one of the most loyal people I know."

"So you guys are friends?" Cookie tried to keep the edge out of her words and mostly succeeded.

"You could say that, yeah." He laughed, but it wasn't his usual warm, rich sound. This was a short, sharp bark, almost a little bitter. "Used to be a lot more than that."

"Oh. I didn't know that." Yep, she could hear the sharpness there, but fortunately Dylan seemed oblivious.

His eyes had gone a little unfocused, evidently seeing something long since past. Something that, judging by his expression, he still missed. She gulped down another mouthful of her drink and thought it really could use more sugar.

"Sure. We dated all through high school, tried to keep it going after, almost got it to work, but..." He shrugged, though there was something off about the gesture, as if he was trying for casual and failing. Opening his mouth, he started to say something else but stopped himself.

"What?" Cookie pressed.

He shook his head, but after a few seconds he leaned back in the chair and met her gaze. In a matter-of-fact tone, he said, "I'd just enlisted, was about to ship out, and thought if I put a ring on her finger, well, then she'd wait for me. She would have. Daisy's like that." He sighed and took a slug of the lemonade as though it were something stronger. "I chickened out, though. We were both way too young."

Averting his eyes, he stared out at the churning sea. "But that was a long time ago."

Cookie was intrigued by these new insights into him as well as a little jealous. She let curiosity win. "Navy, huh?" she asked quietly. "Well, I do love a man in uniform," she joked, trying to lighten the mood again, but the quip fell flat. "I'm sorry," she said instead.

This time his shrug seemed more genuine, if resigned. "That's life, right?" he said to the air around them. "Sometimes things work out, sometimes they don't. Just the way it goes." He finally focused back on her and on their conversation. "But Daisy's not the killer."

"You just said it was a long time ago," Cookie countered. "Maybe she's changed. People do."

"Not like that. She'd never do that." He frowned, the expression pulling his brow down, and suddenly he looked... dangerous. "Who said she would? You said you'd heard her name come up. Wait, let me guess." He let out a snort of derision. "Mindy, right? Mindy Tremaine?" Apparently he read the confirmation in her body language. "Figures. Did she tell you Daisy was one of those mean girls?"

"Something like that," Cookie admitted, even though she knew she probably shouldn't.

"Ha!" He shook his head, not bothering to hide his distaste for the woman. "Trust me, that's the pot calling the kettle—hell, it's more like the pot accusing the teacup of being black. Mindy's the nasty one, got a mean streak a mile wide. She was queen bee in high school, at least in her own head, but Daisy was the one everyone actually liked and looked up to. You know what people used to call them? Betty and Veronica. Like from *Archie*—Mindy was the spoiled one who thought everyone should worship her. Daisy was the hard worker who never realized how hot she was."

"Wow, nice, hard-working, and hot? You're right, you really screwed yourself on that one." Cookie wanted to clap her hand over her mouth, but the words were already out there, and she winced just hearing them again in her head. Why the hell had she said that?

The way Dylan tilted his head to study her, she could see he was wondering the same thing. "Something wrong?" he asked. Then his lips tugged up in a slight smirk. "What, are you jealous of my ex?"

Cookie definitely was. "Why should I be?" she blustered, but she could tell the deflection hadn't worked.

"I don't know," he asked, his tone softer now. "Why should you be?"

"Well, maybe…" She paused but then steeled herself to continue. "Maybe I just want to know that, if we do go out, I won't have to worry about living in her shadow the whole time. Not much point dating you if you're still pining for her."

The chuckle that emerged from him was the one she'd heard that first day, warm and rich and rolling right through her, and it was accompanied by a twinkle in his eye. "So you want to date?" he asked.

Cookie opened her mouth to reply but was interrupted by a shadow that fell across the two of them. A shadow followed immediately by the clomp of large feet up the porch steps and then across the porch.

"Sorry. Am I interrupting?" Hunter asked, swiping Cookie's glass and taking a long sip of her lemonade. He didn't sound sorry at all.

"Would it matter if you were?" Dylan replied,

finishing his own drink and rising to his feet. "Later," was all he said as he stalked over to gather his things to leave. Cookie couldn't tell from the tone if that was a promise or just a standard parting.

When he was gone, she twisted around to glare up at Hunter, who was smirking down at her. "Thanks," she snapped. "Thanks a lot."

"You're welcome." He set down her empty glass. "Now if you're all done flirting with the help, come on. I just got a call from the coroner over in Hancock. He's finished the autopsy and says he's got info for us."

Cookie was on her feet in an instant. "Don't think this is over," she warned as she pushed past Hunter and headed for the stairs.

"Wouldn't dream of it," he answered, and she could hear the laughter in his voice as he followed her out to his car.

12.

"WELCOME TO THE hottest morgue in town," the medical examiner called out as Cookie and Hunter pushed open the doors and stepped into the cool, sterile-looking room, bathed in the stench of formaldehyde. "Where people are just dying to get in!"

Cookie couldn't help it; despite her irritation with Hunter, they exchanged a glance that suggested they both wanted to roll their eyes but were restraining themselves. Oh, this was going to be fun.

"Sorry," their host continued as they crossed the blue-and-white tiled floor to where he sat at a metal desk. "I don't get a lot of visitors, so I like to liven it up when I do. Ha, 'liven' it up, get it?" He chuckled at his own joke.

"You're the one who came and got the body," Cookie noted out loud, studying him. He was tall, only a couple inches shorter than Hunter and a little on the thin side, with short dark hair and the typical olive complexion of a Hispanic. He had a sad-looking pencil mustache, steel-framed glasses, and a nameplate on his white lab coat that read Delgado.

"That's right." He puffed up, clearly pleased she'd remembered him. "Jared Delgado, at your service." Rising to his feet, he took the hand she had reflexively offered, but instead of shaking it, he clasped her hand in his own, rolled it over, and then bent and kissed the back, right above the knuckles. All while gazing up at her.

Oh boy.

"Cookie James," she replied, fighting the urge to yank her hand away. His touch was surprisingly warm for someone who worked with the dead.

"Ah, how fitting," Delgado murmured, obviously trying to be suave. "A sweet name for a sweet lady."

Hunter cleared his throat, forcing the medical examiner to glance over at him instead. "Hunter O'Neil," he introduced himself, flashing his badge. "FBI. Deputy Swan should have told you to expect us."

"Yes, of course." Delgado straightened, finally releasing Cookie's hand, and peered at Hunter. "They say a person's name helps to form who they are, like a self-fulfilling prophecy," he said as he led them over to the far wall with its row of steel doors. "Like parents naming their daughter Joy or Serenity or Hope." He frowned, studying Hunter through his glasses. "Your parents chose Hunter, and here you are, an FBI agent who presumably spends a good deal of his time hunting down criminals, making good on your name. A hunter—

solitary, driven, more at home on the chase than with other people." The way his eyes slid to Cookie made it clear the medical examiner was busy drawing all sorts of conclusions, or at least grasping at them.

"You told Deputy Swan you had information about Chip Winslow," Cookie reminded him, trying to keep her tone friendly but brisk. She didn't really want to invite any additional familiarity with Mr. Delgado.

"Oh, absolutely." He grasped the handle of one door and yanked it open then slid out the tray. The formaldehyde stench intensified, and Cookie tried not to breathe. A sheet-covered body lay there, and the medical examiner pulled back the fabric for them to see the man's face—or what was left of it. The water had twisted his features, leaving them so deformed as to be unrecognizable. Cookie had seen Chip Winslow around the island several times, but even so, she had a hard time reconciling that handsome, if insufferably smug, man with the pale, wrinkled, misshapen face in front of her.

"Winslow, Charles Xavier," Delgado read off a file he'd brought over. "Age thirty-two, permanent residence listed as 12 Terrace Way down in Cumberland. Cause of death…" He paused, looking up at them with a grin.

"Just tell us already," Hunter growled.

Delgado shot him a wounded look, deflating as though someone had stuck a pin in him. "Fine." With a heavy sigh he returned to the report. "Cause of death was a puncture wound to the back of the head. It pierced the skull and the brain, causing a massive embolism. He died instantly." Lifting Winslow's head, he pulled aside the dead man's hair to show them the wound, which was large and gaping.

"So clearly he didn't trip, fall in the water, and drown," Hunter commented to Cookie, who was busy snapping a photo of the wound with her phone. "Scratch Deputy Swan's theory."

She nodded. "And a blow like that to the back of the head—hard to do that one on your own," she pointed out. "More likely it was done to him."

Delgado was looking from one to the other, trying to follow their conversation. "He definitely didn't drown," the medical examiner offered. "There was water in his lungs, but it was all post-mortem."

"Can you estimate time of death?" Hunter asked.

Unfortunately, their host shook his head. "Not exactly," he admitted. "His time in the water messes up a lot of the tests I'd normally run. I can tell you how long he was in the water, though," he offered. At their nod he brightened a little, turning back to his chart. "I'd say thirty two, maybe thirty four hours."

Hunter turned to Cookie. "When did your mother find the body?"

"Around eleven in the morning," she said, remembering. "So that'd place him in the water between eleven p.m. and one a.m. Saturday night."

"And we know he got into it with Rand Friday night," Hunter added. "But that doesn't tell us where he was Saturday." He shook his head, grimacing slightly.

"Rand could've gone after him again," he suggested, though from his tone it didn't sound as if he was buying that one either. Rand was clearly a hothead, but Cookie'd gotten the impression that he was more reactive than active. He'd stepped in when Chip had been hitting on Mindy Friday night, sure, but choosing to go after the man Saturday seemed out of character.

"I can go back over the body, check for any trace evidence I might've missed before," Delgado offered, breaking into the conversation. "Don't expect too much, though. Long-term immersion will have washed away most of it." Jared's eyes widened as he suddenly remembered something. "Wait." A file cabinet drawer scraped open and Jared said, "I have something else for you." He handed a key to Cookie. "Found this in his pocket."

Cookie examined what appeared to be the key to a house before she handed it to Hunter. Considering it could open anything from a home on the island to something on the mainland it was a pitiful piece of evidence.

"Thank you. We'd appreciate anything else you can find," Cookie assured him with a smile. The medical examiner immediately blushed, stood up straighter and tried to push his chest out. Cookie had to force herself not to laugh.

"I'll call you the minute I find anything," he promised eagerly, pointing at the record. Of course they'd taken down Cookie's name and phone number as the person who'd found the body. Great. He also offered

Cookie one of his business cards so she'd have his number as well.

"That would be a tremendous help," Hunter declared, inserting himself between Cookie and the smitten medical examiner and offering his hand to the ME. Delgado shook it, and then Hunter turned away, a firm grip on Cookie's arm as he steered her back toward the exit. "Thank you, Doctor," Hunter called over his shoulder. "We'll be in touch."

They'd barely been outside ten seconds before Hunter glanced over at Cookie with a huge grin on his face. "Looks like somebody's got a wee bit of a crush on you," he said, laughing at her clear discomfort.

She took a deep breath and let ocean air fill her lungs. No matter how many times she'd been in a morgue she still couldn't get used to thinking she was breathing in the dead. "So what?" she shot back. She wanted to deny it, but there was no way. Delgado had made his instant infatuation all too clear. "Are you jealous?"

That only made her ex-partner laugh harder. "Of that little dweeb? Not likely."

"Oh?" She paused mid-retort to analyze his comment. "Not of him, but of somebody else, maybe? Is that why you keep interrupting me and Dylan?"

"Yeah, sure, I'm jealous of a backwoods islander whose only job is helping people paint porches and screw in light bulbs." But there was a bite to Hunter's reply, and he'd stopped laughing, his eyes darkening with something Cookie thought might be anger.

"Dylan's more than that, and you know it," she told him, all playfulness gone. She shook her head. "What do you care, anyway? When this is all over, you'll be going back to Philly."

"You could come back with me." They'd reached his car, and Hunter studied her over the roof of it, his gaze intent and very serious. "Come on, Charlie. This"—he waved his hand at Hancock, which was quaint and peaceful and five times the size of Secret Seal Isle at least, but still felt tiny—"isn't you. You belong in the big city, solving crimes, taking down crooks and fugitives. You're wasting away out here."

"If that's your way of telling me I've lost weight, you need to work on your compliments," Cookie shot back, hands going to her hips, but the quip felt forced even to her. Hunter's words had hit her like a freight train, each word punching its way into her heart.

He was right. She was wasted out here. What was she doing, setting up with her mother and playing at innkeeper? And on a ridiculously small little island to boot? One that didn't even have its own police or medical examiner. A place with a handful of restaurants, no movie theater, precious little in general besides lobster and fish and coastline. This wasn't her. Or, at least, it wasn't Charlene Jamieson. But neither was she, anymore.

"I can't go back," she told him, the words weighing her down like lead. "You know that."

"You mean because of DeMasi?" Hunter asked. "We

can protect you. Come back to the bureau, and we'll—"

"What?" Cookie snapped, anger at least helping her shake off the shroud of depression that had descended upon her. "Put me in protective custody? Babysit me twenty-four, seven? That's crazy, and you know it, Hunter. What'd be the point in going back if I couldn't be out there on the streets, doing my job? If I've got to be hidden away for my own protection, this is a lot better than any safe house." It was her turn to gesture around. "At least here I'm free to roam, to interact, to do things."

"What things?" She could see that he was angry now too, though she wasn't sure if it was at her or just at the situation. "Flirting with the locals? Managing an inn? Fighting with your mother?"

"That's better than nothing," she told him. She kicked a rock, and it skittered across the parking lot. The matter-of-factness of her answer drained his rage away as though someone had stuck a spout in his side. "Believe me, I miss it all like crazy," she continued. "How could I not? Being in the FBI is everything I'd worked for all those years, and I loved it there, Hunter, you know I did. But it's not safe for me. I can't be Charlene Jamieson right now. Maybe not ever again. I don't know. That remains to be seen. But at least Cookie James can try to have some kind of a life, even if it can't possibly be the same." She reached across the car roof toward him, the metal under her arms warm from the sun. "I need you to understand that," she pleaded. "Please."

For once, Hunter abandoned his tough-guy image

and responded, taking her hands in his. "I do," he promised. "I do understand it." A small, sad smile blossomed at the corners of his mouth. "Just don't ask me to like it."

They held hands for a few seconds before he reluctantly let her go.

But as they slipped into the car to begin their trek back to the ferry, Cookie was lost in her own thoughts. Everything she'd said to Hunter had been true. She missed being an active FBI agent like crazy. She also missed Philly itself, with its energy and excitement and all the possibilities there.

At the same time, there were things she'd found to like on Secret Seal Isle. The Salty Dog was one of them. People like Larry were another. The sunsets were glorious, and the coastline really was beautiful. The seafood was amazing. Getting to spend time with Rain, though frustrating, was something she'd been missing out on for years.

And then there was Dylan.

Could all of that offset what she'd given up when she'd left? Maybe. Maybe not. She wasn't sure yet.

But she knew that she was willing to find out.

She also knew, if she was being honest, that the last three days had been the best since they'd moved out here. Part of that had been seeing and spending time with Dylan, certainly. But part of it was being with Hunter again.

And the largest part of it was working this case. This

was what she'd really missed; the thrill of the chase and the sheer joy of going on the hunt.

Clearly, she mused with a smirk, Dr. Delgado's theory about names shaping people didn't always apply. Or maybe Rain had meant to name her something like Hunter, too.

13.

THE FERRY ONLY ran four times a day and took half an hour to get from Hancock to Secret Seal Isle, so Cookie and Hunter had plenty of time to talk over what they'd learned.

Which, unfortunately, wasn't a whole lot yet.

"We need to figure out the murder weapon," Hunter said for the third time after they'd finally driven onto the ferry and were standing at one of the rails, looking out over the water. The engine roared as the boat slowly made its way across. "Until we know what the hell it was, we don't have a snowball's chance in hell of determining who did it."

Cookie had her phone out in a second and pulled up the photo she'd taken at the morgue. "There's no way that's a knife," she pointed out, studying the large, rounded hole. "A chisel, maybe? Or some kind of spike?" She shook her head. "I have no idea."

"Me either," Hunter admitted. "Ask me to guesstimate the caliber of a gunshot wound, and I'll get it right nine times out of ten. But something like this? Who the hell knows?"

"Actually," Cookie replied, a thought occurring to her, "I know someone who just might." She grinned. "But you're not going to like it."

"Who?" Hunter twisted around to see her face and scowled at her expression. "Oh, come on. Seriously?"

"He knows tools," she said. "And that's what we need right now." She frowned at him. "Provided you can check your ego at the door long enough to work together."

"Fine," he grumbled, turning to stare out at the water again. "Go ahead and call him. Let's see if Backwoods Bill can be of some use."

Cookie swatted at him with one hand, already dialing with the other. "Hey," she said once he picked up. "Any chance you can meet us at the inn in about half an hour? There's something we could use your help with." She listened to the reply then said, "Great, see you then." She tucked the phone into her jeans pocket. "He'll be there," she reported to Hunter, who only scowled some more.

This, she thought as she watched the island approach as slowly and inevitably as the tide, was going to be interesting. At the very least.

"WHAT'S UP?" DYLAN asked as he mounted the porch steps. There was a spring in his step and a smile on his face, but both faltered when he caught sight of Hunter standing just to the side of Cookie's seat, arms crossed and face stony. "Agent O'Neil," he continued in a far different tone of voice. "So is this an official questioning?"

"Why? Do you have anything to hide?" Hunter growled back, but Cookie held up a hand to stop him.

"No, of course not," she told Dylan warmly. "Like I said on the phone, we could use your help with something." She patted the seat next to her, the one on the other side from Hunter. "Sit down. Please?"

"Sure." Dylan lowered into the chair but warily cast a glance back at Hunter, who hadn't budged. "What do you need?"

"It's about Chip Winslow, obviously," Cookie explained, since it was clear Hunter wasn't going to be much help. "We know how he was killed, but we don't know what did it. I was hoping you might have some ideas."

"Me?" Dylan tensed beside her. "Why me?"

"Because we think it could be a tool of some sort, and you know tools," she answered. "Would you be willing to take a look at the wound and see if it reminds you of anything? It's a bit grisly, I'm afraid."

Dylan shrugged. "Sure. Can't make any promises, but I'll give it a go."

"Great." Cookie smiled at him.

He relaxed a little, and his chair creaked as he settled back into it.

She pulled the picture up on her phone and handed it over. "That's it."

"Ouch." He stared at the picture but didn't seem sickened by it. Then again, if he'd grown up out here he'd probably seen his fair share of grisly injuries, Cookie thought. Just from what she'd observed, lobstering wasn't exactly the safest profession, and accidents happened all the time. "How big was this hole?" Dylan asked after a second.

"Um, maybe an inch or two across?" Cookie turned to Hunter for confirmation, but all she got was a brusque nod. So much for being on his best behavior. "About that, I think. Sorry. I should've put something next to it for scale, but I didn't think of it at the time."

Dylan continued to study the image. "You could be looking at a hammer," he said finally, "but I doubt it. Most hammers have shaped heads, octagonal or hexagonal or sometimes square for the narrower ones, and those would have left a sharper edge and a more defined hole. This"—he pointed—"looks a lot rounder and rougher, like whatever did it didn't have any facets." He frowned. "Too big to be anything like an awl, and those are made to punch through anyway. The way this is all smashed in, I'm guessing whatever hit him wasn't designed for that. And it hit him straight on, too— there's nothing to the side—so it wasn't a wrench or a pipe." He handed back the phone. "I don't have a clue what could've caused that. Sorry."

Cookie started to tell him that was fine, it had been a

long shot anyway, when behind her Hunter snorted. "Figures," he muttered, just loud enough for them to hear. Both of them.

Dylan was on his feet in an instant. "You got a problem, man?" he demanded, taking a step toward where Hunter loomed.

"No problem at all," Cookie's ex-partner replied, taking care to enunciate each word slowly as if Dylan were impaired somehow. "But this is a waste of my time. Cookie thought you might be able to help. I was never under any such illusion."

"Oh, because us simple folks out here on the island couldn't possibly know anything that Mr. Big City Agent didn't?" Dylan asked, stopping right in front of Hunter now. Cookie saw that the two men were the exact same height, which of course made glaring at each other a lot easier.

"You said it, I didn't," Hunter replied. "But yeah, something like that."

Dylan glared at Hunter. "Anyone ever tell you you've got a bad attitude?" he said, his voice low and intense.

Hunter just gave a tight little grin.

"Attitude like that's likely to end with a black eye and a broken nose," Dylan warned.

That made Hunter push off the wall he'd been half-leaning against and get directly in Dylan's face. "Are you threatening a federal agent?" he asked, his voice soft and cold, his eyes black with rage. "That's a felony."

"Good thing you've got that badge to hide behind,

then," Dylan answered just as intensely. "Wouldn't want to have to face anyone on your own two feet."

"If you want a piece of me, Farmer Bob, I'm more than ready—" Hunter began. But by that point, Cookie was fed up.

"Enough!" she shouted, leaping to her feet and shoving between them, pushing both of them back with one hand. "Stop being idiots, the both of you. A man's dead, and whoever did it is still out there, and you two are standing around here dick-waving instead of doing anything to help."

Both men stared down at her, glowering, and for an instant she felt as if she'd leaped out in front of a pair of raging bulls and was about to get trampled. Then their eyes cleared and both men smiled just a little. They quickly hid their amusement, but Cookie had spotted it and found she could breathe again.

"Dylan, thank you for your help," she told him, turning her back on Hunter. "Even just ruling things out is useful. If you do think of what could've caused that wound, let me know, okay?"

He nodded and turned to go, though he did shoot Hunter a parting glare over Cookie's head.

Hunter started to say something once Dylan had gone, but Cookie held up a hand to stop him before he could even get a word out.

"Don't," she warned. "I'm seriously pissed at you right now, and anything you say is only going to make it worse. Why don't you go take a walk along the shore or something? I don't want to see you before dinner." Then, not giving him a chance to respond, she turned and walked inside, the screen door slamming behind her.

Cookie was still fuming, her feet pounding on the stairs as she ran up to her room. *I need to talk to somebody about all this,* she thought, digging her phone back out of her jeans. She pulled up a number and hit *Call,* then flopped back onto her bed to wait for the phone to connect.

"CJ!" Scarlett's welcome voice boomed in her ear. "Everything okay? When I saw the number I almost freaked!"

That got Cookie to laugh, at least. "Everything's fine," she promised. "Well, no, not fine, exactly. But I'm okay. Personally."

"Oh, that doesn't sound good," her friend said with a sigh. "All right, I'm sitting down. Tell Mama Scarlett everything."

With another laugh, Cookie began filling her best friend in on the events of the past few days. She and Scarlett had first met back in college, when Cookie was studying criminal justice and Scarlett was working on a degree in political science. Although very different in some ways, the two had become fast friends, even rooming together their senior year. They'd stayed close ever since, keeping in touch while Cookie went to Quantico and became an agent and Scarlett went to law school. She was one of the few people who knew where Cookie had gone and how to get hold of her.

"Well, you've certainly been busy," Scarlett commented once Cookie had finished her recap of recent events. "And why am I not surprised that you'd find a dead body out back of your new home? Or at least that Rain would. Sounds like the place is perfect for you."

"Ha ha," Cookie replied, rolling over to prop herself up on one arm. "Trust me, that was the last thing I was looking for."

"Sure," her old friend scoffed. "Come on, I can hear your eyes twinkling from here. You're loving this. You thought you were going into exile out there in the boonies, and lo and behold, a murder investigation falls right in your lap. Almost literally."

"All right, maybe I am having fun with that part of it," Cookie admitted. "And yes, before you ask, it is nice seeing Hunter again. Though he's still just as infuriating as ever." Scarlett had heard all about Cookie's ex-partner and had even been there for Cookie's agonizing bouts of indecision about whether she should go after him or keep it professional. "And now he's being an absolute horror."

"You mean because of this new guy, Dylan?" Scarlett's tone was knowing, and Cookie could practically see her friend's smirk. "He's a real hottie, huh?"

"He is," Cookie agreed with a sigh, closing her eyes to conjure up an image of him. Those eyes, that smile, those strong features—yeah, hot was definitely the word for it. "Though he's not exactly making things easy, either. The two of them were going at it like a pair of dogs trying to prove which is alpha."

"Is it them you're really upset with?" Scarlett asked, her tone going serious for a change. "Or is it just bugging you that you can't decide between them?"

"They're messing up the investigation," Cookie protested, ignoring the nagging voice in the back of her mind that told her Scarlett might be on to something. "That's what's bugging me." She gazed out the window at the vast expanse of ocean and noticed the boats that dotted the horizon, making it look like a postcard image.

"Okay." Her friend didn't sound convinced. "So make sure they both keep their heads in the game, their eyes on the prize, and all that motivational stuff." She paused. "But you are going to have to make a choice, sweetie. The old partner or the hometown hottie. You can't have both. And as long as you leave it open, they're going to keep fighting over you. The sooner you make a clear choice, the sooner the pissing match can end."

Cookie scrubbed at her face with her free hand. "I don't have time for all this relationship drama."

"Nobody ever does," Scarlett said. "That's why it's drama; because it happens at the worst possible time. But you've gotta make room for it and figure it out. And the sooner the better."

"You're probably right," Cookie agreed.

Her friend laughed. "I usually am. Listen, sweetie, gotta go. Catch you later, okay? Let me know how it all turns out. Love ya, bye."

"Love ya, bye," Cookie replied just before the call

ended. Dropping the phone onto the night table beside her, she let her head fall back, the mattress bouncing as she closed her eyes and lay there for a few minutes. There'd be plenty of time later to go downstairs, find Hunter, and deal with him. For right now she just needed a little quiet time on her own.

But try as she might, she couldn't stop hearing her friend's advice. *You are going to have to make a choice.*

14.

THE NEXT MORNING found Cookie eyeing her ex-partner and struggling to keep a grin from plastering itself all over her face. "Guess now you wish you'd brought a different kind of suit, huh?" she couldn't help teasing.

"Shut up," Hunter groused, glaring at her from behind his mirrored shades. "This is ridiculous."

"No. *You* look ridiculous. This is standard procedure, and for good reason." They were making their way along an expanse of rough, slippery, well-worn wooden planks that had been nailed together over long support beams, connected to thick wooden posts as pylons. The island had several different docks, but this one butted right up against the town's main street, and was both the most convenient and the most expensive port on the island. The ferry had a reserved space here, but the rest of the dock was available for both short-term and long-term rentals.

And, as Hunter had discovered after some routine

investigating the night before, Chip Winslow had locked in the use of one particular slip for a period of six months.

Cookie had attired herself appropriately, both for the warm weather and for their destination, pairing cut-off jean shorts with a bikini top and a tied, cropped shirt, plus a pair of rubber-soled water shoes. A baseball cap kept the sun off her face and her hair out of her eyes.

Hunter, on the other hand, was wearing the same dark suit, though with a different shirt and tie. He was sweating in the late-morning sun, and his polished leather shoes kept slipping on the wet planks. He was clearly out of his element here, and Cookie was enjoying his discomfort far more than she should have.

"Let's just find the damn boat and check it out," Hunter grumbled, clutching tightly to the rope strung between pylons as a rough barrier. He let out a string of curses as his foot slid and he grabbed wildly for the rope with both hands to keep from plummeting into the water. The dock tipped precariously with his motions as water splashed over their feet.

"It's at slip number eight," Cookie said, not bothering to hide her laugh. "That should be the next one on our right."

Sure enough, slip eight held a beautiful powerboat, sleek and sophisticated. According to the handsome gold lettering on its side, its name was *Wins Low*. "That's awful," Cookie said, staring at the pun and shaking her head. "A guy like that didn't deserve a boat like this."

"Well, it's not like he can enjoy it anymore," Hunter pointed out. He stepped carefully onto the boat, his feet finally gaining traction on the ridged floor mats. "Come on."

Cookie followed him onto the fancy speedboat. They did a quick canvas of the topside but didn't find anything useful, revealing, or incriminating either up by the pilot's console or back in the lounge area with its comfortable leather seats. "Looks like we're going down," she joked as they headed for the steps leading down belowdecks.

Hunter just groaned.

There were three cabins below, plus a small galley and eating area. Each cabin had its own bathroom, which was a foolish design, but exactly the sort of thing Cookie could see a guy like Chip Winslow insisting on. The main cabin was clearly Chip's, but there wasn't anything interesting there. "A whole lot of condoms, a nicely stocked wine fridge, and some women's clothing that might've been left behind by various conquests or could be some sick form of trophy," Cookie reported after she finally surfaced for air. "But nothing that looks like it ties into his murder or gives away suspect or motive."

Hunter sighed. "I haven't found anything that could be the murder weapon, either," he acknowledged. "This might be a bust."

"I'm not willing to give up just yet," Cookie insisted, giving the cabins one last perusal before returning topside. "There has to be something. If his boat was here

Saturday night—and obviously he left it here before he died, so that would make the most sense—this would be the logical place for him to have been killed. All the murderer would have had to do afterward is to dump the body into the water and let the current carry it away. Only it didn't go far enough. Just around the corner, in fact."

Cookie hopped back onto the dock and was scanning the length of the boat for anything that might fit. As her gaze swept across the vessel, however, something else caught her eye. "Hey, hold on a sec," she called out to Hunter, who was still on the boat itself. "Check this out." She stepped over to where the towline ran from the speedboat to a heavy metal cleat screwed onto the dock. The cleat was shaped like a very short, very broad double T, with two thick stems leading down to a solid base and up to a very wide head that tapered a little and arced up toward the ends. Ends that were roughly circular and perhaps two inches wide.

"Whoa," Hunter answered as he studied the cleat. "I think you've got something there, Charlie." He leaped back over to the dock with a thud and crouched down beside the cleat then compared its end to Cookie's picture of the wound on her phone. "Yeah, you've definitely got something."

Pulling her phone back, Cookie retrieved a business card from her shorts pocket and typed in the number. "Hello, Dr. Delgado?" she said once the call connected. "It's Cookie James."

"Ah, the lovely Miss James," the Hancock medical examiner responded. "Lovely to hear from you. But please, call me Jared. How are you?"

Cookie rolled her eyes but answered, "Good, thank you. I was wondering if I could show you an image and you could compare it to the wound in Chip Winslow's head?"

That got his attention. "Absolutely," he replied. "I haven't had any luck here in trying to figure out what caused it."

"Great, thanks. Hold on, I'll send it to you." Her camera clicked as she snapped a photo of the cleat's end. She texted it to Delgado and then redialed. "Did you get it?" she asked straightaway. "Yes? Good. What do you think?"

"I think that could be the very thing," Jared agreed. "Nice work, Ms. James! Any chance you could bring me the cleat itself so I can make certain? Unless you have the materials on you to make a casting from it."

Cookie frowned. She didn't have any casting materials at all, which she suspected he knew. "We'll see what we can do," she said. "Thank you, Doctor." And she hung up.

"He thinks this could be it, too," she told Hunter. "But he wants us to bring him the cleat so he can be sure."

Hunter nodded. "Makes sense." He studied the heavy metal fixture. "I can try to pull it free, but I'm not sure how much luck I'll have. It looks pretty solidly attached."

Cookie laughed. "Sure, you could give that a shot, He-Man," she agreed. "Or we can try it the easy way." The metal of her Leatherman was warm in her hand as she pulled it out of her back pocket.

"Where the hell have you been hiding that?" Hunter asked, grinning at her. He held out his hand. "Let me have it, and I'll have this thing off in a jiffy."

Cookie frowned and swatted his fingers away. "Let you have it? Why should I? I was the one smart enough to bring a tool with me—I get to be the one to use it." She flipped the Leatherman open and pulled out the screwdriver attachment on one of its arms.

But when she reached toward the cleat, Hunter got in her way. "Come on, Charlie," he said, gripping her arms to stop her. "Yes, you thought to bring it, that's great. But I've got a lot more muscle than you do. I'll be able to get the cleat loose a lot faster. Do you really want to stand around out here in the hot sun ten times longer just because your pride won't let you admit that?"

"Ten times longer?" Cookie pulled away. "Gee, thanks for that high opinion of me, Mr. Macho. I'm not some delicate little flower, remember? I may not be Miss Muscles, but I'm pretty sure I can get the job done, and it won't take all day. Now move!" She was starting to get pissed off—she'd always hated it when he got condescending.

Especially because he was so stubborn about it. "Fine, I'm sorry," he said, though he didn't sound the least bit contrite. "Maybe it wouldn't be ten times as long. But it would take longer, and I'd prefer to get the thing over to the ME as soon as possible. Wouldn't you?"

"Sure," Cookie agreed. "So stand aside and let me at it." Then she hip-checked him out of her way.

Unfortunately, when she did that he stumbled, his shoes slipping on the dock yet again. And he windmilled his arms, reaching out desperately for anything that could keep him from falling.

Anything—like Cookie.

His arms wrapped around her. But of course Hunter was bigger and heavier than she was, and although her shoes gave her decent traction on the slippery wood, they didn't anchor her against his weight tugging her sideways.

She flailed back, trying to free herself but only succeeding in pitching both of them forward... and right off the side of the dock, narrowly missing the back of the *Wins Low*.

Sploosh!

They hit the water hard, sending a great wave of it back up onto the dock. The impact tore the two of them apart, and the cold shocked Cookie alert. She'd always been a strong swimmer, and it only took her a second to kick back up to the surface, her head breaking through at the same time Hunter's did. The icy temperature sucked the air from their lungs, and they both came up gasping.

"You okay?" he asked Cookie, even though he was

the one wearing the suit and dress shoes.

"Yeah, sure, I love taking a quick dip in freezing ocean water every morning," she shot back, reaching up to tug her soaked cap off her head and brush back the heavy mass of her sodden hair. "You?"

"Stunned, soaked, and freezing," he admitted, "but otherwise, yeah." Reaching up, Hunter managed to grab hold of the boat's anchor line, tugging it down a little. With his other hand he reached out for Cookie. "Here, grab hold, and I'll pull us both in."

Though she knew she had more range of movement than he did, Cookie also realized that she probably wouldn't be able to grab the rope on her own. So she complied, taking Hunter's free hand and letting him reel her in. Both their clothes were soaked through, of course, and plastered to their bodies, so when Hunter pulled her up against him Cookie discovered she could feel every inch of him through their various layers.

Every inch.

She licked her lips, suddenly glad the water around them kept things cooled off as saltwater stung her tongue. At the same time, she was embarrassed to realize that he must be feeling every inch of her too. And that her nipples had already gone hard from the cold and were now poking into Hunter's chest.

Perhaps he'd noticed that as well, because he was suddenly motionless, his arm still wrapped tightly around her.

A violent shiver shot through both of them. A beat

went by as they stared at each other, then Hunter shook himself out of his daze. He flexed the arm clutching the rope. "Put your arms around my neck," he instructed, and Cookie did so, trying to ignore the way that molded her to him even more tightly.

Hunter smiled down at her, his eyes dark with desire, but then concentrated on using both arms to haul them back to the dock. They'd only landed a few feet out, though now it felt like miles. When they were against the dock again, Cookie grabbed the cleat with both hands and pulled herself up and out of the water. The planks of the dock were hard on her ribs as she lay there gasping from the effort and cold. She barely managed to roll to the side before Hunter was flopping down beside her.

"Right," he said after he'd caught his breath. "Let's not do that again."

Cookie looked over at him, lying there in his ruined suit, and when the ridiculousness of the situation hit her she started giggling. She couldn't help it. He frowned, then sighed, then began chuckling as well, and in seconds both of them were lying there, stretched out on the dock, laughing uncontrollably.

Which, she decided, was probably better than thinking about the fact that they had been caught in such a tight embrace just seconds before. She was still flushing from the close contact and knew from their clinch that Hunter hadn't exactly been immune to it either. She carefully chose not to glance down at him to confirm that fact. Who knew that hugging someone while fully clothed in the freezing water could feel so… intimate?

To take her mind off the embrace, she rolled over and eyed Hunter wryly, keeping her gaze on his face.

"So," she said, propping herself up on one arm. "Can I unscrew that thing now, or do we need to take another dip to settle this?"

He just grinned back at her and waved an arm weakly in the direction of the cleat. "Be my guest."

She rolled her eyes and looked around for the Leatherman, which she'd dropped when they'd toppled over.

As she began unscrewing the heavy cleat, she tried to ignore Hunter's eyes on her… and the fact that her clothes were so skintight they might as well have been painted on.

At least with her bent over the cleat, he couldn't see her face. No doubt it was flaming red from embarrassment—and desire.

15.

"**I** LOOK RIDICULOUS," Hunter groused as he stomped out onto the inn's front porch.

"If you'd thought to pack more than one outfit—" Cookie started, but he cut her off.

"Give it a rest, all right? This is your fault. If you hadn't let your mother near my running clothes, I could've worn those. But now that she's managed to somehow shrink them two sizes in the laundry, that's out of the question. Besides, I already told you I was in a hurry to leave and my other suits were at the dry cleaner's. Not to mention, I didn't realize I was going to be here for more than an overnight. You seriously don't have any other clothes I can wear?"

"Oh, sure," Cookie replied, rolling her eyes, trying to keep the mental image of him in his too-small sweats firmly out of her mind, "I just keep a bunch of men's clothes on hand. For my many nighttime guests, dontcha know?" Then she got a good look at her ex-partner and burst out laughing. "Aw, you look adorable!" she managed to gasp out between guffaws.

"Ha ha. Laugh it up," he grumbled. "I'm glad somebody's enjoying this."

"We really don't have anything else," Cookie assured him, wiping tears from her eyes. "You're lucky the previous owners left some things behind. Otherwise you'd be in my mom's dress right now."

The inn's previous owner had left a box of cast-off clothes in the closet under the stairs, presumably items forgotten by former guests over the years, but many of them were much too small for a man Hunter's size. Which was why he was now standing in front of her wearing a pair of pink-and-purple-flowered Bermuda shorts and a giant-sized navy T-shirt that read 'Fishermen Make A Great Catch' over a pair of crossed fishing rods. Lime-green flip-flops completed the picture. "Maybe you should add a tie," Cookie suggested before cracking up again.

"I'm still armed, you know," Hunter pointed out. "Don't make me shoot you." While he'd never been a particularly funny guy, he normally did have at least some sense of humor. Of course, he also took his appearance very seriously, so dressing like this was a huge blow to his self-image. But Cookie was enjoying his discomfort. Considering how many times he'd made her feel awkward or embarrassed already during his visit, it was nice to have the flip-flop on the other foot for a change.

"Good luck drawing from under that tent," she

replied, still chuckling. "But if you're done with your little fashion show, we need to get this"—she hoisted the cleat they'd taken from the dock—"back to Jared."

"How could I forget?" Hunter muttered as he marched toward his car. "I bet he'll get an even bigger kick out of this than you do."

"WOW!" JARED EXCLAIMED when he saw them, his eyes lighting up at the sight of Hunter's new get-up. "That is some outfit. What, did you lose a bet?"

"No, but it turns out that FBI suits aren't drip-dry," Cookie replied before she giggled. The whole way there she'd had a hard time keeping a straight face, and she'd lost it every time someone else on the ferry had smirked in Hunter's direction. "You're going to be the talk of the town," she'd told him after one couple snapped his picture. He'd actually tensed as though he was going to go after them and rip the camera from the man's hand, but Cookie had held him back.

"Glad I can give back to the community," he'd growled, but at least he was back to being snarky again. She considered that a good sign.

"Oh, I see." Surprisingly, the medical examiner stopped laughing and eyed Hunter with some sympathy instead. "If you want, we've got a box of old clothes over there," he said, gesturing toward a table against the room's far wall. "Taken from the bodies, of course, so you'd want to wash them before wearing any of them, but you could probably find a… less colorful ensemble, at least."

Hunter's eyes widened and his mouth hung open for a moment, shocked by the ME's suggestion. "Thanks," he said after composing himself. "I'll take a look in a minute." For now, however, he gestured for Cookie to do the honors.

"Ta-da!" she declared with a flourish, digging the heavy metal cleat out of the bag she'd carried it in. It made a hollow thud on the metal examining table when she set it down, and Jared bent over it to inspect the object.

"I'll need to measure it, of course, and make a mold, but I'd be willing to bet this is your murder weapon." He straightened back up and asked, "Where did you find it?"

"The deceased's boat was tied to it," Hunter replied. He was frowning, but Cookie knew that look. He wasn't annoyed, just simply trying to put the pieces together. "If Winslow slipped," he pointed out, "and fell backward, onto that cleat—"

"It would have pierced his head at exactly the right angle," Jared confirmed. "Yes. And the impact would be more than enough to do the kind of damage he incurred."

"So it could have been an accident," Cookie chimed in. "I mean, that dock was pretty slippery, right, Hunter?" She couldn't resist getting in that little dig.

"It was," he agreed, ignoring the jab for now. "Though I'd assume Winslow was more used to it than I am and had more appropriate footgear. Still, anyone can slip." He focused on the medical examiner. "Did you find anything else?"

"A few things, actually," Jared said. He all but beamed with his apparent success. "First, the deceased did not have any recent bruising, pre- or post-mortem, aside from right around the wound itself. He had a few older bruises, I'm guessing a few days before his death, but nothing newer."

"So he wasn't in a fight," Hunter concluded.

The doctor held up a finger. "Ah, but he did have bruises and contusions along the knuckles of his right hand," he added, "and those were right before his death. So he may not have been punched—"

"But he punched somebody," Cookie finished for him. "Got it." She shook her head. "That pretty much rules Rand out. There's no way Chip got in a punch on that guy and didn't get beaten down in return."

Hunter nodded. "Threw a punch but didn't take one sounds like either he got one in by surprise or he hit somebody and laid them out with the first blow." He glanced at the wall of steel doors that housed the cadavers, and one Chip Winslow. "Dude was decent-sized," he said after a second, "and looked like he probably exercised some, but he was hardly a bruiser like Rand. So for him to nail somebody hard enough to put them down with one punch, it'd have to be somebody pretty flimsy. A little guy—"

"Or a woman," Cookie interjected, saying what she

knew they were all thinking. She was big enough and sturdy enough that a guy like Chip Winslow might not be able to knock her out with one punch, but plenty of other women wouldn't have been so lucky. And cocky rich guys sometimes didn't like being told no. "Mindy didn't have any visible bruises," she offered, remembering their interaction with the stylist.

"Could've used makeup to cover them up," Hunter pointed out. "We're also talking about Saturday night, and it's Friday now, so she'd have had more than a few days to heal up." He rubbed at his jaw, thinking. "We know she flirted with Chip, and we know that Rand threatened Chip because of it. Maybe she went down to Chip's boat Saturday night to patch things up, afraid of losing her big tipper? But Chip wanted more than she was prepared to give. She said no, he hit her, she shoved him back, he fell, hit his head, and died?"

"Plausible," Cookie agreed. "And then she dumped the body in the water, hoping to get rid of it, but instead it washed up at my back door. Crap luck for her."

"Worse for him," Hunter reminded her, and Cookie nodded. She hadn't liked Chip much—nobody had—but he hadn't deserved this.

Jared had been watching the exchange silently, eyes wide as if he were seeing something amazing happen right before him. Maybe he was, Cookie realized. This was when she and Hunter were at their best together, bouncing ideas and theories around, playing off each other's hunches and instincts. It was why they'd been such a good team, and she could barely stand how much she'd missed it.

Jared cleared his throat. "I did find something else," he said slowly. "Something that might help you narrow down your field of suspects." He had their full attention as he got up and moved to his desk, where he retrieved a plastic evidence bag. It rustled as he brought it back over and handed it to Cookie, who peered inside it. The bag held a small, crumbly yellow hunk of something roughly triangular in shape.

"What is it?" she asked, tilting the container and studying the way its contents shifted. "It looks a little bit like—"

"Brick," Jared answered proudly. "It's a fragment of a yellow brick. I found it caught in the cuff of his pants. Best guess? Whoever dumped him in the water weighted him down with yellow bricks, hoping the body would sink and never be recovered. But they weren't tied on tight enough, or they were old and disintegrated in the water, or something caused the bricks to come loose, which is why he floated away instead."

Hunter took the bag from Cookie and shook it. "A yellow brick?" he asked, staring at it. "I didn't think that actually existed outside of the *Wizard of Oz*."

Cookie slapped him lightly on the arm. "Don't be a tool," she warned. "Just because they don't have them in Philly doesn't mean they don't exist anywhere else. It's a big, big world, you know."

"Yeah, well, most of it isn't worth seeing," Hunter

shot back with a sharp grin. Apparently he'd gotten his sense of humor back after all.

Jared seemed less than amused. "We may not be a big city like Philadelphia," he declared huffily, "but that doesn't mean you can go demeaning us." He snatched the bag from Hunter's hand. "Do you even know why someone around here would have bricks on hand?"

Hunter stared at the geeky medical examiner, as if stunned that someone so clearly not his physical equal would dare to get in his face like that, but after a minute he shook his head. "No idea," he admitted.

Cookie, however, already had the answer to that particular question. "It's for lobstering," she said, turning to Jared for confirmation. "Right? Lobstermen use bricks to weight their traps."

"Exactly," the medical examiner told her triumphantly. He bestowed a smile on her that said he might be even more smitten now. "It's the easiest, cheapest, simplest way to make the traps sink down to the bottom, where the lobsters crawl about. And when a brick cracks or crumbles, you just toss it and get a new one." He frowned at the bag he held. "It's mostly the mineral content that determines color. Add a lot of iron, and you'll get pink bricks, for example. Yellow or white usually means more lime. You don't see a lot of yellow bricks around here. Most are the standard red and brown, so it shouldn't be too hard to find out who uses these."

"And whoever it is would have a supply of them in

his boat," Cookie added. "So it'd make sense to use them when trying to weigh down Chip's body."

"Exactly." Jared shot a glare at Hunter. "Maybe if the FBI took the time to learn more about what goes on in backwoods towns like this one, their agents would know about this stuff, too."

Cookie held her breath for a second, not sure how Hunter would take that. It was entirely possible he'd fly off the handle at the little medical examiner, especially considering his ego had already taken a few hard hits today. But instead her ex-partner surprised her by nodding thoughtfully.

"You're right," he told Jared without a trace of sarcasm or condescension. "That's really good information and a subject I knew nothing about. Thank you for all your help, and I'm sorry if I insulted you or your town." He offered his hand.

Jared stared at Hunter for a second, then down at his hand, then back up at him, clearly speechless. Finally, he took a few steps and shook hands with him. "Yes, well, don't worry about it," he offered. "I'm sorry I got a little hot under the collar. I get a tad bit defensive when I think someone is putting us down."

"You had every right to call me on my behavior," Hunter replied. "I'm sorry." The corner of his mouth quirked up. "In my defense"—he gestured down at his clothes with his free hand—"I might have had a reason for being short-tempered myself."

That actually drew a laugh from the coroner, and not

a mean one. "Fair enough," Jared agreed, any animosity toward Hunter apparently forgotten. "And I'm glad I could help." He glanced over at Cookie, an unmistakable puppy-dog look on his face. She could practically see his tail wagging.

"You've been a huge help," she assured him as she pulled out her phone and snapped a photo of the yellow brick fragment.

A dopey smile claimed his face as his metaphorical tail waved back and forth all over the place.

Hunter stalked over toward where Jared had indicated the box of cast-off clothes lay, leaving Cookie to face Jared on her own.

"My pleasure," the medical examiner told her cheerfully. He turned a bit red in the face. "Perhaps, sometime, you might like to… have dinner with me? After all of this has been settled, of course."

The cardboard box of clothing scraped along the floor as Hunter dragged it closer and pretended to be solely focused on the contents. Cookie knew she was on her own. "Oh." She had been afraid that was coming. He seemed like a nice enough guy, and she didn't want to hurt his feelings but decided it was best to just be honest right from the start. "I'm flattered, really," she told him, "but I don't think that would work. I'm sorry."

"Ah." He deflated right before her eyes, all but sinking back into his chair. "No, I understand."

Hunter returned to her side, a bundle of clothes clutched in his hands. "We should get moving," he told

Cookie, who nodded quickly. "Thank you again," he told Jared, patting the devastated coroner on the shoulder.

Jared lifted a hand in a halfhearted wave good-bye, but he didn't bother to look up as they left. Cookie reminded herself it had been the right thing to do, telling him no before he could get his hopes up.

But she still felt awful all the way home.

16.

"STOP BEATING YOURSELF up about it," Hunter advised, shaking Cookie out of her funk. They'd managed the return trip and were now back on the inn's front porch, lemonade in hand, her phone sitting on the little side table between them displaying the photo of the yellow brick. The house key gleamed in the sun beside it. "You let him down easy instead of leading him on. That was the right thing to do."

Cookie shrugged, annoyed both that she was still upset about her interaction with Jared and that Hunter had correctly read the cause of her concern so easily. "He seems like a nice guy," she said, more to herself than to her ex-partner, "but I just... there wasn't any..."

"Spark?" Hunter offered, something beyond sympathy in his tone, and when she glanced up at him, she saw that he had one of his customary smirks plastered across his face. Ice in his glass rattled as he sipped some of his drink. His eyes had darkened, however, suggesting that perhaps he wasn't taking this conversation as lightly as she'd suspected.

But she couldn't deny the truth of his statement. "Yes," she agreed finally, picking up the phone to study the photo without really seeing it. "There wasn't any spark." She knew without looking at him that Hunter was leaning in toward her a bit more, and exactly what he was pointing out without actually saying it. Yes, the two of them had plenty of sparks.

Jared had clearly noticed, and Cookie was sure that was part of why he'd gotten so defensive at Hunter's crack about how small-time Hancock was. Her mom had seen it right away. Others had spotted it as well. She cringed as she recalled a meeting with the agent in charge of the Philly field office shortly after she'd started there, warning her that she and Hunter would have to be careful to remain completely professional and to not "let any mutual attraction interfere with their working relationship."

The only problem was she'd never been sure if sparks were all they had. After all, strike two pieces of metal together, and you'd get a spark. That didn't mean they were a match, just that there was friction and a physical connection.

And she'd always been careful not to broach the subject while they'd worked together. If they'd tried something and it hadn't worked out, well, they'd still have been stuck as partners. Talk about awful. And if it had worked out? Their boss had been right—it would have clouded their judgment when on the job.

Then she'd moved away. And now Hunter was here, but not for much longer. Which made the idea of trying to start anything both ridiculous and dangerous, even if she thought they could have more than wild attraction. Why take the risk of exploring it if it would just be torn away a few days later?

And was he really the one she wanted, anyway?

Argh, enough of this, Cookie thought, shaking herself free of her wild notions. She set her phone down with a clatter and picked up the key. The edge was rough on her palm as she fiddled with it. They had a job to do, and right now that should be her focus, not all of… this. She picked up her phone again and forced herself to stare at the photo, to actually see it this time.

"We need to figure out who uses bricks like this," she said aloud, trying to drag her attention back to the matter at hand. "We can head down to the docks and check out the lobster boats there as they come back in for the day. Maybe we'll get lucky and see them without having to ask any questions—or produce any warrants."

Hunter frowned beside her. "You really think it'll be that easy?" he asked, accepting the change in topic without comment. "These guys strike me as the don't-take-to-outsiders-much type, and I'm definitely an outsider." He was still wearing his get-up from earlier while the clothes he'd found at the coroner's were being washed, and the give-me-a-break-here look on his face made Cookie laugh, which was a welcome relief.

"No, you're not exactly going to blend in," she

agreed, unable to prevent a smile from touching her lips. "You'll have to let me do the talking."

She knew that irked him, but he bowed his head, acknowledging the necessity.

"We still have the key to consider too," Cookie said.

"What are we going to do with that?" Hunter asked. "Test it on every door in town?"

Just then, Rain emerged from the house, a pitcher of lemonade in her hands. "You need to test a key? I'm pretty handy with inserting things into slots." Her wink at Hunter made Cookie groan as Rain added, "Maybe I could help."

"It's not that simple, Mom," Cookie said.

"Oh." Rain smiled and lifted the pitcher. "How about a top-off?" she offered, stepping over to them. "And we've got booze inside if you need it a little stronger."

"Just lemonade would be great, thanks," Cookie replied, holding up her glass.

Liquid gurgled as Rain refilled both glasses. Then she glanced down at the phone. "What's that?"

"A piece of yellow brick," Hunter answered. "Might be evidence." He sipped his lemonade. "Thank you, Ms. James."

Rain waved a hand at him. "It's Rain, please," she said, unable to resist flirting. But she was still staring at the photo and frowned. "You know what that looks like?" she said finally. "The bricks at the Salty Dog. They're the same color as that."

Cookie gaped at her mom. "The Salty Dog? What bricks?" Then it hit her. Rain was right. Most of the building was weathered wooden shingles, but the base of the building was a layer of brick, and they were the same yellow as the one Jared had found. "Oh, wow," she muttered.

Hunter was watching her closely. "The Harrises?" She could tell by his tone that he sympathized, and when she met his eyes they were a warm brown.

"The Harrises," she agreed slowly. She didn't want to admit it, but it was hard to deny the evidence. "They have their own lobster boats—that's where most of their lobsters come from for the restaurant, and Larry buys off the other lobstermen to supplement as necessary. I know because I've heard him complaining about it once or twice." She sighed. "And if they have these bricks lying about from building the place—"

"They'd use them in their traps rather than waste them," Hunter finished for her. "Yeah."

"So I was helpful?" Rain asked. She'd remained hovering over them during this last exchange.

"Yes, Mom," Cookie told her honestly. "Very helpful. Thanks."

Her mother nodded and left without another word, which was strange in and of itself. But she was beaming as she departed, and Cookie was glad that at least one good thing had come from the revelation.

"Okay, let's talk this out," Hunter suggested quietly. He didn't sound too excited about it either, and Cookie appreciated that, recognizing that it was only because he knew she liked Larry. "We've got just the three of them, right? Larry, Daisy, and Stone."

Cookie nodded. "Yeah. They've got people working the boat, of course—I've no idea who they are—but they wouldn't have as much at stake as the Harrises themselves."

"Right." Hunter rubbed a hand over his smooth scalp, as he often did when he was thinking. "And Chip didn't show any signs of bruising except for around his knuckles, so he wasn't in a fight, or at least not one where the other person hit back." He grimaced. "Maybe it's chauvinist of me to say it, but I'd pretty much rule out most guys from that."

Cookie had to nod. "The lobstermen tend to be tough," she agreed. "And Chip's no Rand. One blow from him isn't going to knock them out, and they'd have hit back, absolutely. Same with Larry." She considered. "I don't know about Stone. He's kind of a lightweight and more a toker than a fighter. But he grew up around here, so I wouldn't be surprised if he could take care of himself despite all that."

"That leaves Daisy," Hunter pointed out. "What do we know about her?"

"Loyal to a fault," Cookie replied, remembering what Dylan had said with a sharp pang. "Bit of a temper. Would do anything for her family." Each word made it sound worse and worse.

She could see that Hunter felt so, too. "So we've got

Chip, who wants to buy Larry's restaurant out from under him," he said, thinking it through out loud. "We know he likes the ladies and comes on strong. Daisy confronts him down by his boat, tells him to back off her dad. He hits on her instead. She gets pissed, maybe takes a swing at him. He hits back reflexively, even though she either didn't connect or didn't do any damage. She shoves him. He falls backward, hits his head, dies. She freaks, decides to dump the body. Drags it into her family's lobster boat, weighs it down with some of the bricks they've got lying about, manages to tip him into the water. The bricks pop loose, he floats up and away and washes ashore." He studied her. "What do you think?"

Cookie considered it from every angle. Her phone was slick in her hand as she stared at the picture of the brick while she turned Hunter's theory over in her mind. "It holds up," she finally forced herself to say. "She's got motive, certainly. And means." She shook her head. "I think we don't have a choice. We've got to bring her in."

"Yeah." Hunter glanced up at the darkening sky. "Bit late for it now. Let's go get her first thing in the morning. I'll call Deputy Swan and make sure we can use the station. We'll interview her and see if she slips up."

"And check for telltale bruises," Cookie added, though she knew that was a longshot. It had already been enough time that any such marks could have faded. But maybe they'd get lucky.

So why was there a pit in her stomach, making her

slightly nauseated? They finally had a real suspect, and she felt worse than ever. But if she was honest with herself she knew why. Dylan had spoken up for Daisy. It was obvious that even if their relationship was long since over, he still liked her. And Cookie liked him. Enough that she didn't want him to think less of her. Which he definitely would once he found out she'd arrested his ex on suspicion of murder.

But Cookie knew there was no way out of it. Not now. Not with the brick pointing them right to Daisy. They had to follow the evidence, no matter what. Even if they really didn't like what it was telling them.

17.

"**W**E'RE ALL SET," Hunter told Cookie later that night. After dinner he'd disappeared to make a call, and now he joined Cookie out on the porch, waving his phone at her. "Deputy Swan said he'll be ready in the morning. Plus, he called the judge in Hancock—who it turns out is another cousin, go figure—and we'll have a warrant in the morning, giving us the authority to search the Harrises' boat."

Cookie nodded. "Even if we do find the yellow bricks, that's not proof," she pointed out as he sank into the chair beside her. She indicated the thermos on the table in front of them, and the empty mug beside it.

Taking the hint, Hunter scooped both up and then poured hot coffee from the one into the other. Cookie had her own mug firmly clasped in both hands as the rich aroma filled her senses.

"I know," he agreed after taking an appreciative sip. It had cooled down outside just enough for the steaming hot beverage to really hit the spot. "But you know as well as I do that it's one more link in the chain." His eyes twinkled. "Or should I say, just another brick in the wall?"

She groaned at him and swatted his arm. "I guess you got your sense of humor back," she joked, sipping her own coffee to hide her smile. "Must be the change in attire."

"It's hard to find anything else funny when you're the one who looks like a joke," Hunter confirmed with a chuckle. Before dinner, he'd changed into some of the clothes he'd gotten from Jared. Though they weren't anything fancy, and certainly weren't up to his usual standards, the tan slacks and blue pullover looked both more comfortable and a lot less silly than what he'd been wearing earlier.

"I guess now you know to bring a spare change of clothes next time you come to visit," Cookie shot at him. Then she bit her lip as she heard the words out in the open.

Beside her, Hunter raised an eyebrow. "The next time?" he asked, his voice dropping several octaves to a deep rumble that thrilled her to her bones. "So you think I'll be back?"

"Oh, I know you can't stay away," she countered, her own voice gone throaty as well. Why did she do this to herself, she wondered, twisting a length of hair around her fingers as she watched Hunter watching her, his eyes dark and serious.

"You may be right," he murmured and leaned in

toward her. "I just can't seem to quit you, Charlie."

She shifted in her own chair, angling toward him as well, her eyes trapped by his hungry gaze, her lips parting slightly, her breath coming heavier, every muscle in her body taut, every sense alert, every nerve on fire—

"Uhhhhh."

Startled, Cookie jerked away, but Hunter looked just as surprised. Then the sound came again, and she realized it wasn't emerging from him at all but from somewhere around the side of the inn.

"What the hell?" Hunter snapped, rising to his feet. Cookie was right behind him, and as one hand automatically set down her coffee mug the other fled toward the gun she had holstered at the small of her back. The heavy weapon was firm in her hand, and her ex-partner had drawn his as well, she noted as the two of them moved carefully and with as little noise as possible across the creaky old porch to the front stairs.

"Where's your mom?" Hunter whispered as they both crept along the front walk and then onto the lawn, trying to figure out where the noises were coming from.

"Out," Cookie replied. "She said she was going for a walk after dinner. She likes to stroll along the beach and look at the sunset." She glanced over at Hunter, who was peering into the dusk, trying to track the guttural sounds that continued to float toward them. "You think this has something to do with Chip Winslow?"

He shook his head but didn't glance her way. "I don't know," he admitted, gun still out but aimed down at the ground, ready to rise in an instant. "Can't imagine how. We assumed his body washing up here was a coincidence, but what if it's not? What if it's got something to do with this place—or with you?"

A sudden wind knifed through Cookie, chilling her to the bone, even though the night air was perfectly still. *Something to do with you.* Could it? Had DeMasi tracked her down somehow? Was Chip Winslow some kind of twisted warning? She shook her head, trying to dispel the paranoia. If they'd wanted to send her a message, they wouldn't have used someone she barely knew and didn't particularly like. But some of that fear had taken root, and she was horrified to see that her gun was shaking slightly in her hands.

And still the sounds continued.

"Uhhhhh. Uhhhhhh." They sounded as though someone might be in pain, and Cookie's blood chilled further.

"They're coming from over there," Hunter whispered, gesturing with his gun toward a small storage shed sitting to one side of the house. "Who has access?"

"Everyone," Cookie replied just as quietly as they inched closer. "It's not locked." She shrugged at his surprised glance. "What? It's got some spare lawn chairs, a beach umbrella or two, stuff like that. Who'd want to steal it?" Hunter shook his head, and Cookie felt a flash of irritation at her ex-partner. This wasn't the big city, and he needed to understand that. Things were different out here. People were different out here. Which didn't in any way explain what really sounded like grunts of pain emanating from the shed.

"Ohhhhh. Uhhhhh. Damn!"

At that last one, which had been scratchy, deep, and male, Hunter finally launched into motion. Covering the remaining distance to the shed in two long strides, he raised his pistol with one hand and grabbed the shed door with the other. Then, checking to make sure Cookie was behind him and off to the side slightly so that she had a clean shot, he yanked the door open. It crashed against the building.

"Freeze, FBI!" he shouted, his second hand flying forward to steady his gun as he trained it on the shed's occupants. Cookie did likewise, targeting even as her mind took in the new details being sent from her eyes:

The inside of the shed. Chairs and cushions and other paraphernalia.

Two figures. One straddling a chair. The other straddling the first. Facing each other.

Jeans. Down around the first figure's ankles.

A dress, hiked up over the second figure's hips.

A familiar tie-dyed dress.

A very familiar person wearing that dress and now peering over her shoulder, mouth open in surprise.

A less familiar bearded face gaping at them in shock.

Then Cookie was lowering her gun and turning away, her free hand flying to her face in an attempt to block out what she'd already seen and could never unsee, no matter how hard she tried. "Geez, Mom!" she burst

NEW CORPSE IN TOWN

out. "What the hell?"

"What?" Rain replied. She lifted herself off the man with a giggle, her dress fortunately sliding back into place as she moved. The last thing Cookie needed right now was her mother giving her ex-partner a peep show.

Her partner! Cookie slid her gaze over to Hunter, who stood as if frozen, his face locked into an expression of utter surprise. "Hunter?" Cookie asked softly, resting a hand gently on his arm. "You okay?"

With a shudder he finally tore his eyes from the scene before him and spun about to face her. "Yeah, fine," he managed to choke out, and if Cookie hadn't been so mortified herself she'd have laughed. She hadn't even known his face could turn that shade of red. "I'll leave this for you to straighten out," Hunter rasped and stalked away into the darkness, holstering his pistol as he went.

Cookie sighed and put her own weapon away, turning back around to confront her mother, who was now exiting the shed, leading her male companion out by the hand. He'd taken the time to pull up his pants, Cookie was glad to see.

"Really, Mom?" Cookie managed. She shook her head. "In the storage shed?"

"Oh, you know what they say," her mother replied cheerfully. "Any port in a storm." She giggled again. "And Anthony here certainly wasn't complaining about my port, were you, Anthony?"

Anthony, who Cookie thought she recognized

vaguely, muttered something and scuffed the ground with the toe of one boot. His face was bright red behind his beard.

"Anthony's a lobsterman," Rain continued as if she were introducing them during a casual walk about town. "He was just coming off his boat as I was walking by. We got to talking, and then, well, to other things. This seemed like a good place, quiet and private, and I didn't want to disturb you and Hunter in the house." Another bubble of laughter burst from her. "I guess we got a little loud, huh?"

Cookie opened her mouth to reply then shut it again. She honestly had no idea what to say. Instead she turned and walked away, looking for Hunter. She found him pacing the front porch. "They still out there?" he asked as she approached.

"Yeah, but probably not for long." She sighed. "Look, about that—"

But Hunter held up a hand. "I don't ever want to talk about that again," he told her. "Ever. Okay?"

She almost laughed but managed to swallow it. "Sure," she agreed instead. "Forget it ever happened."

"Right." He still sounded a little strangled as he grabbed his now-cold coffee, gulped it down, and then retreated to the house. Cookie watched him go. So much for whatever had almost happened between them just a few minutes ago.

Replaying the recent events in her head as she gathered up the thermos and her own mug, Cookie debated what to do about Rain. Her mother was getting more and more out of control. First the dead body, which hadn't been her fault. Then scaring away their first paying customers by toking up with the wife. And now banging one of the locals in the storage shed.

Cookie was starting to get a little worried about what her mother might do next. She needed someone to keep an eye on Rain, she decided. And she couldn't do that herself, at least not until they'd solved this case. But who else could she trust? She considered Dylan but immediately dismissed that idea. She still wasn't sure where they stood, exactly, and although she did like him, Cookie had to admit there were a lot of things she didn't know about the man. Plus, he had a vested interest in the case, so asking him to watch over Rain would be risky. He'd be right on top of them all the time and might stumble upon some confidential information.

There really was only one person she could ask. Cookie pulled her phone out of her pocket and, for the second time in a matter of days, dialed a familiar number.

"Gee, miss me?" Scarlett teased as she picked up. "What's going on? Did you make a choice already? Good for you, girl!"

"It's not that," Cookie answered and could practically hear her best friend shifting gears at the tone in her voice. "I need to ask you a favor. A big one."

Her friend didn't hesitate for a second. "Name it," she replied. "You need somebody rubbed out? Because

I've got connections."

That at least made Cookie laugh. The only "connection" Scarlett had was to her favorite restaurant, and only insofar as they had her credit card on file and knew her favorite dish and her preferred wine to accompany it. "Nothing quite like that," she said. Then she sighed. "It's my mom."

All banter vanished from Scarlett's voice in an instant. "Is she okay?"

"She's fine, but she's getting out of hand." Cookie recounted the shed incident, which made her friend laugh. "I'm worried that she's going to get herself in trouble. I was wondering, I know it's a ridiculous thing to ask, but is there any chance you—"

"Could come out for a visit and just incidentally keep your mother from doing anything crazy?" That was one of the great things about being friends for so long— Scarlett had known exactly what she was going to ask. The other great thing was that she immediately followed up with, "Of course, sweetie. I never use my vacation days, and my desk is pretty clear right now, so why not. I'm on the next flight out. See you soonest, love ya, bye!"

"Love ya, bye," Cookie responded, feeling much better as they hung up. Rain might be a force of nature, but so was Scarlett, and if anyone could keep her headstrong mother in check, it was her equally stubborn best friend. Plus, it would be nice to see Scarlett again, regardless of the reason. And maybe, Cookie admitted to herself, she could also get her friend's firsthand take on the whole thing with Hunter. And the maybe thing with Dylan. Cookie groaned and headed inside. When had life on a quiet little island gotten so complicated?

18.

THE NEXT DAY was Saturday, and it certainly started well. Though Cookie had of course gone to bed alone again, never even considering propositioning Hunter after what they'd both seen the night before. What was it with her mom exposing herself to the men in Cookie's life, anyway, she wondered?

She'd at least gotten a good night's sleep out of it and was awakened by the rumble of a car pulling up out front. She only dimly registered the slamming of the vehicle's door, a woman's laugh, and the sound of a departing engine. But she came awake fully at the sudden shout of, "Hey, what does it take to get some service around here!"

She knew that voice. "Scarlett?"

For half a second Cookie thought she must be dreaming. What would her best friend be doing all the way out here? But then the memory of last night's phone call resurfaced. And then she was bolting out of bed and leaping down the stairs, taking them two at a time. Good thing she'd fallen asleep in yoga pants and an oversized T-shirt.

"Scarlett!" Cookie flung open the front door, barreled across the porch and down the steps, and wrapped her arms around her friend. "You made it!"

"Of course," came the reply against her ear as her friend returned the embrace. "Told you I would, and when have I ever let you down?" Before Cookie could even answer, her friend was laughing again. "Oh wait, do not mention that double date again," Scarlett added. "That was years ago."

"And I'm still scarred," Cookie retorted, letting go and pulling back so she could stare her friend in the eye. "Deeply, deeply scarred. He offered to give me a free breast exam. Right there in the restaurant."

"I know, I know." Her friend sighed. "They were med students. I figured 'hey, future doctors.' I didn't know it also meant 'hey, potential creepers.'" She studied Cookie, a smile on her face. "You look good."

"You too." But then, Scarlett always looked good. She was gorgeous like a model, a force to be reckoned with during lawsuit negotiations, and the years had only given her face more character. Wearing a black silk top and matching slacks that set off her pale skin and ash-blond hair nicely, she peered out from beneath her wide, straw sun hat, the perfect picture of the dazzling urbanite spending a day at the beach.

"Where's the fire?" A deep voice rumbled behind her, and Cookie glanced back to see Hunter emerge from the inn—and couldn't help but stare a little. It turned out he slept in yoga pants, too. And nothing else. Damn.

"Well, hello, handsome," Scarlett all but purred, gliding past Cookie and extending a hand. "You must be Hunter. I'm Scarlett, CJ's oldest and best friend."

"Pleasure." Hunter reflexively shook hands, his eyes doing a quick assessment. Cookie was still doing some assessing of her own. She'd always known Hunter was well built, but wow. He put most male models to shame. "Wait, her oldest friend?" She glanced up as she saw him put some pieces together. "So you knew where she was?"

"Of course," Scarlett answered. "We don't have any secrets from each other." Which was pretty much true. Scarlett was like the sister Cookie had never had, if that sister was her age, her best friend and closest confidante, and a genius with clothes and makeup.

She saw Hunter process that information, almost managing to hide a brief flash of hurt. "And you're here now because—?"

Cookie decided to spare her friend from further interrogation. "I called her last night," she explained, wrapping an arm around Scarlett's shoulder. Her friend's perfume filled her nose with a sexy spiced scent that Cookie was sure was the latest "it" brand. They were the same height, though Cookie was considerably curvier. "I asked if she could come out. I figured it'd be a good idea for someone to keep an eye on my mom."

"As long as that someone isn't me, that sounds great," Hunter agreed, wincing at the recollection. Then his eyes widened. "Wait, where did you come from?" he demanded. "She just called you last night, and you're already here? What'd you do, fly?"

Scarlett laughed. "Didn't you?" She took off the sun hat and fanned herself with it, her green eyes sparkling with mischief. "I took a flight from New York to Bristol then hired a chopper to get me from there to Hancock. From there, I paid a very nice fisherman to bring me over in his boat, and then talked some nice young man into giving me a ride up here from the docks."

Cookie couldn't help but chuckle. Scarlett had always been a bit of an unstoppable force. And she was incredibly good at getting men to do what she wanted. The fact that her law firm was doing well probably didn't hurt either.

Hunter was shaking his head in awe. "Wish I'd come up with you," he muttered. "Would have saved me a lot of time."

The look Scarlett shot him could have boiled an egg. "I bet you do," she said with a wicked grin. "But anyway, we're all here now. So what's for breakfast? I'm starved."

With unusually good timing—probably because she was no doubt desperate to know all about the new arrival—Rain appeared just then and announced, "Breakfast!" before disappearing back inside.

"There you go," Cookie told her friend, hugging her again and then reaching down to grab the small valise standing beside them. "Food, and you get to see Mom again. Two for the price of one!" She hoisted the heavy suitcase up the stairs.

"Careful dear, you're making it sound like a bargain sale, and you know how I feel about those," Scarlett replied. They both laughed as they headed inside, Hunter trailing behind them looking more than a little overwhelmed. *Poor boy,* Cookie thought. Between her and Scarlett, he'd never know what hit him.

THE REST OF the day, unfortunately, looked to be a bit less pleasant, though hopefully just as productive or even more so. After breakfast, Cookie ran upstairs, showered and changed, and then she and Hunter headed over to the Salty Dog. They left Rain and Scarlett chatting about makeup and clothes and homemade salsa recipes.

"Do we know what she looks like?" Hunter asked as they entered the restaurant. Conversations hummed as silverware clashed, signaling a busy morning crowd. Her partner was again wearing the slacks he'd gotten from Jared, but with one of his button-down shirts and a tie, appearing professional enough. As long as no one looked down and saw the flip-flops.

Cookie frowned. "Not really," she admitted. "I usually come in on Wednesday, her normal day off. But apparently she's hot, so she shouldn't be hard to find." It wasn't a very big island, after all.

Stepping inside, she was still blinking to adjust from the sunlight when a friendly female voice declared, "Hi, welcome to the Salty Dog. Two for brunch?"

Blinking more rapidly, Cookie squinted enough to make out a pretty redhead standing before them, a pair of menus already in her hand. Late twenties to early thirties, wearing little to no makeup, and her hair pulled into a simple ponytail, she was dressed in jeans and a tied-off button-down but still looking amazing. "Daisy Harris?"

The woman beamed at her, and Cookie could easily see why Dylan would have been smitten and why Mindy would consider her such a threat. The expression took Daisy from lovely to stunning, as if pure sunshine were leaking from every pore. "That's right. Have we met?"

"We haven't," Cookie replied. She held out her hand. "I'm Cookie James. My mother and I bought the Secret Seal Inn." She indicated Hunter beside her. "This is Agent O'Neil with the FBI. And I'm really sorry about this."

"Sorry about what?" Daisy started to ask, but she barely got the question out before Hunter stepped up, looming over the poor girl.

"Miss Harris, I'm going to have to ask you to come with us," he told her, his voice and manner all business. "We need to speak with you down at the station regarding the death of Chip Winslow."

"Uh…" Daisy looked completely confused, but fortunately she didn't resist, and called for her father to take over her duties before Hunter led her away. Cookie followed, shooting an apologetic look at Larry while he watched with helpless concern. When they were back outside, they walked toward the deputy station.

Cookie did her best to keep up with Hunter's quick pace, but with every step her spirits sank a little further. She had a bad feeling this was only going to get worse.

"I'M TELLING YOU, I didn't do anything to Chip Winslow!" Daisy insisted for the third time, slapping her hand on the desk. "Or with him, or around him, or anything. I barely knew the guy. Sure, I've seen him around, and I know he kept pressuring Dad to sell him the Salty Dog, but everybody knew that was never going to happen."

"He never hit on you?" Hunter asked coolly. "I find that hard to believe." Clearly he'd noticed her charms as well, Cookie thought with just a little heat.

Daisy flushed at that. "Yeah, okay, whenever I saw him he did the whole slimy come-on thing, but so what?" She shrugged. "I blew him off, he went away, rinse and repeat. That was as far as it went, and as much as I ever thought about it. Or him."

"When was the last time you saw him?" Hunter inquired next.

Their chief suspect frowned. "I don't know," she admitted after a few seconds. "Last week some time, I think. Wednesday? Thursday? Could have been Friday, even. He'd come round the restaurant yet again, urging Dad to sell. He made some sleazy comment to me, and I told him to get lost." Another shrug. "He did. That was it."

Cookie set her phone in front of Daisy, open to the photo of their chief evidence. "Does this look like a piece of one of the bricks used to build the Salty Dog?" she asked.

"Aren't you just an inn owner?" Daisy asked. "Why should I answer any of your questions?"

Hunter cleared his throat. "Ms. James has a law enforcement background. She's working for me temporarily. Consider any questions she asks as official questions of the FBI."

The fact that he had to explain away Cookie's presence, made her bristle. The FBI had been her identity for so long, it was hard to just be an "inn owner."

But the explanation seemed to pacify Daisy because she shrugged and studied the image. "Could be."

"And where were you late last Saturday night and early Sunday morning?" Hunter pushed.

"At home," Daisy told him. "With Dad and Stone. Then asleep—alone. Then at the Salty Dog, getting set up."

Cookie and Hunter exchanged a glance. It was a weak alibi at best, no one but immediate family around, and they couldn't be trusted not to cover for her. They couldn't see any obvious bruises, but that didn't mean Daisy hadn't healed enough to conceal them. She still had means, motive, and possible opportunity. She'd certainly given them nothing to exonerate her.

Just then Cookie's phone started to play Love Shack. Her mother's smiling face flashed on the screen, and Cookie groaned, wondering when her mother found time to change her ringtone. After last night's activities, no doubt. The song was a little too much even for Rain. Though she should have ignored it, Cookie ground her teeth and answered with a bark, "You're out of control."

"No, I'm brilliant. I solved the mystery of the key. You're never going to guess whose it is," Rain said.

"Mother!" Cookie admonished and turned away from Hunter and Daisy, lowering her voice. "You stole the key? What were you thinking? That's evidence. And where's Scarlet?"

"Don't worry about her. She's enjoying some much needed hammock time. Just listen. I was out taking my walk and killing two birds with one stone. And I figured out who it belongs to."

Cookie sucked in a sharp breath, torn between wanting to scream at her mother or kiss her. "And?"

"It's for Daisy's apartment." Rain's tone was full of pride and superiority. "I told you, you'd never guess."

Unfortunately, Rain's discovery fit Cookie's theories all too well. "Mother, you should not have done that. But now that you have, thank you for the information. Please wait for me at home, and whatever you do, don't go into Daisy's apartment."

"Of course not, dear. That would be an invasion of privacy." Rain clicked off and Cookie signaled to Hunter.

After filling him in on Rain's call, Hunter rose from his seat. "Miss Harris, I'm afraid we're going to have to hold you for further questioning," he informed her. "I'll have Deputy Swan formally charge you with suspicion, and the Hancock judge may set bail, but I'm guessing you won't be going anywhere for a while." Then he stepped out of the room, holding the door open for Cookie to join him.

"Can we really hold her?" she asked as soon as the door had shut behind them. "It's still circumstantial."

"Enough to charge her, at least for now," Hunter replied, though he sounded unsure as well. "Hopefully that'll give us the time to find real proof."

Cookie nodded but wasn't thrilled about it. Daisy didn't seem like a murderer. What if they had the wrong person?

"WHERE IS SHE?" a deep, rough voice demanded, and Cookie immediately tensed. Spinning around, she saw Dylan striding toward them across the deputy's station.

"If you mean Miss Harris, she's in custody," Hunter replied, moving to intercept before Dylan could reach Cookie or the door behind her that led back to the cell where they'd just placed Daisy after the judge had faxed over the warrant for her arrest. "And unless you're her legal counsel, you can't see her."

"The hell I can't," Dylan snapped, shifting to go around Hunter. Cookie winced, knowing what a mistake that was.

"Back off," Hunter warned, his own voice dropping to a much lower register as his body tensed for action. When Dylan kept coming, Hunter's arm shot out, hand open and at a right angle, clearly intending to shove Dylan back by the shoulder.

Only, Dylan slipped past the blow, grabbing hold of Hunter's wrist with one hand, his other rising to slap Hunter's opposite shoulder. The next thing Cookie knew, Hunter was leaping back up from where he'd hit the ground, his eyes gone flat black and his face murderous.

Whoa. Cookie had seen her ex-partner take down all sorts of bad guys, including ones with a whole lot of combat training. She'd never seen him take a fall before.

Who was Dylan, exactly? He'd said something about enlisting—had he been special forces or something?

Right now, though, she had a more immediate concern. Namely, how to keep the two men she was interested in from killing each other right there in the sheriff's office.

"Okay, stop!" she shouted, stepping forward and raising her hands as she attempted to slide between them. Two equally rock-hard chests were under her palms as she pushed them apart. "Enough!" That at least made them both pause. "Look, let's just talk this out," she insisted, eyeballing each of them in turn. "Okay? Before somebody gets hurt."

"I'll tell you who's going to get hurt," Hunter

growled. "It's Mr. Fix-it over here."

"Not likely," Dylan shot back, matching Hunter glare for glare. But when Cookie pushed harder against his chest, he let her shove him back another step. She did the same to Hunter, and at least now there was a little space between them.

"You're holding Daisy," Dylan ground out after a few seconds of staring. "Let her go. Now."

"That's not going to happen," Hunter answered. "Not unless you've got a hundred K lying around for bail."

Cookie wasn't entirely sure how he'd gotten the judge to set bail at such a ridiculously high amount. But she was even more shocked when Dylan unslung the gym bag she'd only just realized he was carrying and dropped it onto the nearest desk. "One hundred thousand," he announced. "Now let her go."

Stunned, Cookie stepped over to the bag, unzipped it, and looked inside. Sure enough, it was filled with cash—bundles of hundreds, counted and tagged by a bank. Five thousand per bundle, the bills rustled as she confirmed that there were twenty bundles. "He's not kidding," she told Hunter. "He's just posted bail for her."

Hunter's scowl could have frozen a forest fire, but there wasn't anything he could do about it. "Fine," he said finally. "Go get her."

This time it was Cookie who wouldn't back down. "No, you go get her," she replied. "I'll get Swan to fill out the forms." *No way am I leaving the two of you alone in here without adult supervision,* she added in her head, and she was fairly sure the thought was strong enough that her ex-partner picked up on it. That earned her another glare, but finally Hunter turned away and headed for the cells.

When the heavy door slammed shut behind Hunter, Cookie said, "Look. I'm sorry. We had to—"

He raised a hand to stop her. "I really don't want to talk about it right now," he told her gruffly. "Just show me what to sign and where so I can take Daisy home."

That made Cookie bridle a bit. Home? As in, his home? Her home? *Their* home? But she ground her teeth together, bit her tongue, and went to find Swan. By the time Hunter was back with Daisy, everything had been filled out, signed, and squared away.

"Dylan?" Daisy asked as soon as she caught sight of him. "What're you doing here?" She sounded genuinely surprised.

"Bailing you out," he answered, his tone thawing a bit. "Your dad called me, told me they'd brought you in. Something about Winslow having a key to your apartment."

Her eyes narrowed in disgust. "I never gave that to him. The creep must've stole it last week when he was at the Salty Dog, the same day I lost my keys." She gave an involuntary shudder. "It never occurred to me someone would've taken them."

Dylan leveled a death-stare at Hunter. "Take those

off her," he insisted, clearly meaning the handcuffs.

The chain rattled as Hunter removed the cuffs from Daisy's wrists then stepped back and watched without a word as Dylan led her out. At the door, Dylan stopped long enough to look Cookie's way, but she couldn't read his expression.

His eyes were gray as steel, though. And just as cold.

19.

THE NEXT MORNING, Cookie surprised herself by rising at dawn, pulling on a pair of bike shorts and a T-shirt, and creeping downstairs and outside. Though not normally big on morning exercise, she needed to get out, stretch, and do something active.

Especially if it would help her erase yesterday's events from her head. Like the way Dylan had looked at her as he'd escorted Daisy out.

"We did what we had to do," Hunter had insisted after the pair—were they a pair? Cookie had found she really wanted an answer to that question—had left. "She's our chief suspect. We had no choice."

"To bring her in, yeah, sure," she'd agreed. "But to charge her? Maybe. And then to set bail at a hundred thousand? She's not exactly a flight risk. Her entire life is here on this island, and it doesn't provide a lot of hiding places."

"It was enough that I figured her dad couldn't leverage the restaurant to cover it," Hunter had

x

explained, finally calming down. He'd been ready to go after Dylan for a rematch, and Cookie had known that wouldn't have ended well. "That was all. I just wanted to keep her here, sweat her a bit, and see if she let anything slip." He'd slammed one hand down on a desk. "I didn't expect the handyman to show up with a gym bag full of cash." The look he'd leveled at her then had been sharp, serious, and devoid of the usual macho rivalry. "Charlie, how much do you really know about this guy?"

Not a lot, Cookie admitted to herself as she walked away from the inn, slowly increasing her pace until she finally broke into a steady jog. Her muscles flexed tightly with the movement, but she knew that would pass once she'd warmed up. Dylan Creed. Born and raised here. Left for college, he'd said, though he hadn't said where, or what his major had been, or even if he'd graduated. He'd said he'd enlisted when he was eighteen. She suspected in the Navy, though she didn't know for certain, nor did she know how long he'd been in or how and why he'd left the service before starting college then coming back here and starting his own business. He had his own place—apartment or house, she wasn't sure.

And evidently, he had a hundred thousand dollars just sitting around. Oh yeah, and could toss Hunter around as though he were a wadded-up napkin. Also, Dylan was insanely hot, smart, engaging, fiercely loyal, more than a little bit of a flirt, and good with his hands. She tried not to dwell on all the implications of that last statement.

Her mental musings had brought Cookie into town, and she slowed as she glanced around, making sure she wasn't about to drift into traffic. It was still early enough, though, that most regular folk were still in bed. The lobstermen were already out on their boats, of course, checking their catches even as the sun came up.

But as she turned down the main street, Cookie did spot one other figure awake and outdoors at this ungodly hour. Curious, she jogged a little closer. It was a guy, she saw, decent height but rail thin, dark hair that might have been black or brown or even a deep red. He was wearing jeans and a plaid shirt over a T-shirt and was carrying a cardboard box. As she approached, she saw him shove the box into the back of an old Subaru parked there at the curb.

It was the Subaru that clued her in as to who she was looking at. "Good morning!" she called out, picking up her pace in order to close the remaining distance quickly. Stone Harris, brother of Daisy and son of Larry, started at the greeting and glanced up, suspicion naked on his narrow face. He looked a little like Daisy and a little like Larry, Cookie thought as she came to a stop just a few feet from him, but without the drive and determination that showed so clearly through both of them. "How's it going?"

"Uh, good," Stone replied, shoving his hands into the pockets of his jeans. He scuffed the ground with his worn sneakers, stole a quick peek at her face, which then tracked down across her body, then glanced back down at the ground again. "You?"

"Oh, can't complain," Cookie replied as she leaned on her thighs to catch her breath, her chest heaving from her run. "You're Stone, right? Stone Harris?" She cut him off before he could ask. "I know your dad a little bit. Love the Salty Dog."

"Yeah, it's great," Stone agreed, still not looking at her directly. "Uh, they should be opening up soon. If you hurry, you can get the first biscuits of the day. Dad makes 'em fresh."

"I know. They're so good." She realized she was laying it on a little thick, but something in her warned to keep him talking. She glanced at the battered Subaru beside them, and the boxes filling most of the back. "Wow, early bird gets the worm, huh? What's with all the stuff?"

"Camping trip," he replied, though she didn't see a sleeping bag or a tent at all. There was a scuffed blue cooler on the front passenger seat, but most of the other stuff looked more like personal items than camping gear. Who brought a box of old photos when they went camping? And not just photos, but framed ones, as though he'd just pulled them off the wall?

"Really?" she asked. "I didn't realize there were any good places for camping around here. Where do you go?"

When he squinted at her, she knew she'd pushed it a little too far. "Who are you, anyway?" Stone demanded, finally looking her in the eye. "I don't know you."

"Cookie James," she replied, holding out her hand. "My mother and I took over the Secret Seal Inn."

"Ah, yeah, right." He shook hands with her, though he seemed to do it reluctantly, and he pulled his clammy hand free as soon as he could. Nervous? "Well, nice to meet you." His eyes—the same green as Daisy's, she noted—darted over to check out her rack again. Yuck.

Cookie decided it was time to drop the act. "Look, Stone," she said, her hands going to her hips, "don't do this." She waved at his heavily laden car. "Whatever it is. Daisy needs you right now."

"What?" He was staring at her again, only now it was confusion and anger rather than lust. "What do you know about any of that?"

"I know that she was formally charged with manslaughter," Cookie responded. "I know that she posted bail. And I know they're still looking for that last little bit of evidence, the one that'll put your sister away for good." She shrugged. "If it was my sister facing all that, I'd want to stick around. To be there for her."

"Yeah?" He barked out a short, bitter little laugh. "Lady, trust me, the last thing Daisy needs is me around. She'll be a lot better off if I'm out of the picture. And speaking of being out—" He slid past her and closed the car trunk with a solid thunk. "I've got a few more things to take care of. Nice to meet you." Turning his back on her, he retreated to a small apartment building just past where she'd first seen him.

Cookie watched him go, regretting there wasn't

anything she could do to make him stay. She was just a civilian. But Hunter was a whole other matter. She pulled out her phone and hit Call. "Where are you?" she demanded as soon as he picked up his phone.

"Back at the inn. Why?" he said. "Where are you? Is something wrong?"

"I'm in town," Cookie answered, glancing back the way Stone had gone, but she didn't see him returning yet. "I just ran into Stone Harris. He's got what looks like half his life shoved into his car, and he's grabbing the last few boxes now." She paused. "I think he's doing a runner, Hunter. We can't let him disappear. I have a feeling he's the one we need to crack this case."

"Could be," Hunter agreed. "If nothing else, he may know something about Daisy, something damning."

"Or he could be our guy," Cookie argued. "He's not exactly buff. I get the feeling any punch he throws has the word 'tropical' before it, and the word 'rum' after that."

"Okay, I'm on my way." She could hear rustling before the pounding of what she suspected were his feet on the stairs. "See if you can stall him."

"I'll try." Cookie hung up and slid the phone back into her shorts just as Stone re-emerged with another box.

"You again?" he groaned as she moved to intercept him at his car. "Just leave me alone."

But Cookie shook her head. "Not really an option," she replied. "Come on, Stone, help me out here. What really happened to Chip Winslow? If Daisy's the one who killed him, why are you the one who's running?"

She tried getting between him and his car, but he just stepped around her. And, when she wouldn't move away from the trunk, Stone reached out and shoved her to the side, not meanly but hard enough that she stumbled back a step.

"Just get out of my way," he half-pleaded, half-urged. "Okay? Let me go." He opened the trunk wide enough to insert that box with all its fellows then closed the trunk again and walked around to the driver's side.

As he pulled open the driver's door, his eyes met Cookie's for just a second.

She'd seen lots of different eyes over the years. Some were angry, some were elated, some were confused, some were vengeful.

Stone's were haunted. With guilt, if she wasn't mistaken. Enough guilt to leave him washed out and haggard. It was the look of a man who'd done something he shouldn't and understood that there would never be a way to make amends to all those who had been harmed.

Then he blinked and glanced away, breaking the connection.

Should she take him down, Cookie wondered. She could—though not on Dylan's level, or Hunter's, she'd had the training. Used it more than once out in the field, too. And a few times off-duty when some guy at a bar had gotten a little too free with his hands. It wouldn't be hard to put Stone down on the ground and keep him pinned until Hunter could get there and take him into custody.

But if she did that, as an ordinary citizen, it could screw up any case they had. A decent lawyer could claim that she'd interfered, maybe even get her for obstruction or some sort of entrapment, and get anything they wound up learning from Stone after that thrown out of court. Better not to take that risk. Which was why she stood back and watched without a word, as Stone Harris climbed into his little Subaru and the car rattled away.

And standing there on the sidewalk as the Subaru's taillights faded into the morning mist, Cookie could feel it in her gut that she might also be watching her entire case go up in smoke.

20.

HUNTER PULLED UP in his rented Mustang two minutes later.

"Where is he?" he demanded as Cookie hurried around to the passenger side and all but leaped into the slick, black muscle car.

"He got away," she answered. "He'll be heading for the ferry. Hit it."

She'd barely gotten the door closed when her ex-partner punched the gas, peeling out with a loud screech and a deep thrum.

"Got away?" he asked as he took the next left, sharp enough that Cookie grabbed the handle over the door to keep from being flung about like a rag doll. "How'd that happen? He pull a gun on you?"

"No, he didn't do much of anything." She sighed, glancing out the window as the small town zipped past. "I'm not an agent anymore, Hunter, remember? I can't arrest him. If I had, I could've given an attorney an excuse to bounce the case."

She watched his jaw tighten before he nodded. "Yeah. Good thinking." He followed the compliment by slamming his palm against the dash, making her jump. "But damn! I wish I'd been just a little quicker."

"Then catch him."

Hunter pushed down harder on the gas, sending the heavy sports car roaring forward like a lion in full charge.

But when they screeched around another corner and came into view of the main dock, both of them stared in surprise.

There was no sign of Stone or his Subaru.

But Cookie's initial thought—that they'd missed him and he'd already made it safely onto the ferry—shredded as she realized there was no sign of the slow-moving boat either. And the water here was smooth enough that you could literally watch the ferry the entire way from the mainland to the island and back again.

Squinting, after a few seconds she stabbed one hand forward, pointing at something out on the water. "There!"

It was the ferry, all right. It had to be.

But it was moving slowly toward them, not away from them.

Hunter let out a breath. "So we beat him here." Then he frowned. "How *did* we beat him here? This car is fast, and I'm one hell of a driver, but he had a head start. And he knows these roads—what there are of them. He should be down there on the dock, waiting."

Cookie considered that. "Unless he knew he'd never

get to the ferry in time," she replied. "We've only been here a few weeks, and Mom and I are already starting to memorize the ferry's schedule. The foghorn sounds off as it reaches the dock. It's like church bells or the town clock or something. Everybody knows it, and you can set your watch by it. Stone's lived here his whole life—he'd know the ferry was still at least ten minutes out. And if he guessed that we'd be after him—and he's a petty drug dealer, he's got to be paranoid—he wouldn't let himself get caught out on the dock like that."

Hunter twisted about to face her more fully. "All right, then," he asked, his features sharpening. "So where did he go instead?"

But to that question, Cookie had to shake her head. "I don't know. There aren't any other ways off this island. That's why we picked it. You take the ferry, or you're stuck."

"There has to be something," Hunter argued. "Something we just aren't seeing. Or don't know about because we weren't born here."

His statement made Cookie glance up at him. "I do know someone who could help with that," she said slowly. "But I doubt he wants to hear from me right now. And there's no way he's going to want to help you with anything."

Hunter's frown darkened into a scowl as comprehension struck. "Oh, come on!" he demanded. "Him? There's got to be somebody else."

But she was shaking her own head, even as she pulled

out her phone and dialed. "I haven't really met too many people yet," she explained as she raised the phone to her ear. "There's Larry, but I think we can both guess how that would go." The call connected. "Hello, Dylan?"

"What do you want?" Though not the harshest greeting she'd ever received, it wasn't too far off, the tone cold and utterly businesslike. Cookie found she had to swallow before she could go on.

She clenched her eyes shut and massaged a temple to stave off the low-grade headache that approached. "Look, Dylan," she started, "I'm sorry about all this. I really am. What little evidence we've got so far pointed us pretty solidly toward Daisy. We had to bring her in and see what she said for herself."

"Yeah?" The lone word dripped with scorn and disbelief. "That why you charged her with Winslow's murder? I *told* you she didn't have anything to do with it."

"You did," Cookie agreed, her own tone heating up as anger surged through her. "But it's not like I could just take your word for it. You used to date her, for God's sake! You're hardly impartial. And the evidence pointed her way." She reined in her temper, focusing on the task at hand. "Hers… or Stone's."

That got his attention, at least. "Stone's?"

"Stone's," Cookie repeated. "Only problem is, the little stoner split on us. I caught him packing up his car, but the ferry's still on its way over, and Stone is nowhere to be found." She paused. "We need your help, Dylan.

Please."

His short, sharp bark of laughter echoed in her ear. "Are you for real right now? You accused Daisy of murder, now you want to blame her brother as well, and you want me to help you catch him? Dream on."

But Cookie wasn't ready to give up. "Think about it," she urged. "If Stone's behind this, he's leaving his sister to take the fall for him. And if he's not, well, why did he run?"

"Because he's a stoner, and typically paranoid," came the reply. "On top of which, he's basically the closest thing this island has to an actual drug dealer. If he caught even the slightest whiff of cops or feds, he'd be nothing but a memory." Dylan still sounded annoyed, but maybe not as much. His tone didn't seem as harsh or as closed off as it had been before. Unless she was mistaken, she was starting to get through to him.

"If it's just about some pot or some acid, he's got nothing to worry about from us," Cookie insisted. "We're only after whoever did Chip in. You told me that wasn't Daisy, but it could be Stone. We can't be sure until we catch him and question him, though. *If* we can catch him."

She could hear a faint rushing sound and realized it was Dylan scratching at the stubble along his chin as he thought—the way she'd seen him do when he was considering a project at the inn. Who knew such a sharp little noise could be so enticing? And what would it feel like to run her own fingers over that stubble, along that strong jawline? She repressed a shiver. Fortunately, he spoke again before her daydreams could run away with her.

"I might know where he went," Dylan admitted. "You're down by the main dock, right? Watching the ferry?"

"That's right."

"And you're in that black Mustang that's been parked at the inn the last few days?"

So much for being inconspicuous, Cookie thought, though she did get a warm jolt from realizing he'd been keeping tabs on her for at least the last few days, maybe longer. That had to be good, right? The fact that he couldn't keep his eyes off her? Or was it just the natural inclination of a small-town native to wonder about anything new and unfamiliar?

"Yes, black Mustang," was all she replied. Best not to make a big deal out of it. "You?"

The sudden rap on the passenger's-side window startled her, and she jumped in her seat, one hand clutching the phone and the other diving back behind her to latch onto her gun. But then she saw Dylan's face peering at her through the glass, grinning. Ah.

"Let him in," she told Hunter as she hung up her phone. He scowled and glared and kept both hands firmly on the steering wheel. "Hunter, let him in," she repeated firmly. "We need him."

"Fine," Hunter finally grumbled, popping the locks. "But if he pulls a gun on us or something, don't blame me."

"Morning," Dylan said as he opened Cookie's door, waited for her to climb out, and then squeezed into the car's incredibly cramped backseat. "Doing a little sightseeing, eh?"

Cookie reclaimed her seat and turned, noting the gleam in his eye. He'd gone from pissed to mischievous in one point six seconds flat. What was he up to? Playing along, she asked, "Sure, why not? Anything you think Hunter here really ought to see?"

"Well, there's one place," Dylan answered, drawing out the words just to make them suffer. Cookie could tell he was enjoying himself. "It isn't open right now, strictly speaking, but it's still a nice place to sit and relax, and it's got a gorgeous view. Good enough to paint, even."

Cookie had been puzzling over his words, trying to make sense of them as he spoke, and she could see by the knit of his brows that Hunter was just as confused as she was, if not more so. But then she registered Dylan's last comment, and something clicked in her memory. A slow smile spread across her face as she turned to her ex-partner.

"I know where Stone went," she told him. She hoped she—and Dylan—were right.

21.

"EXPLAIN THIS TO me again," Hunter insisted as he gunned the engine and raced down the island's main street, flying past their one tiny post office, the sheriff's station, and the handful of other businesses and organizations. "The only way off the island is the ferry, and the ferry only stops at the main dock. The one we just left. But instead of waiting there for Stone to show, you've got me speeding away from it, to the other end of this place." His gaze flickered briefly toward the backseat, then toward Cookie before returning to the road as his grip tightened on the steering wheel. "How do we know you're not just creating a diversion, getting us out of the way so Stone can make a clean getaway?"

"Because," Dylan snapped back before Cookie could even formulate a reply, "the one I'm worried about here is Daisy. And like Cookie said, if Stone is behind this, he's leaving her in the lurch. I won't stand for that." He sighed and rubbed at his face, once again eliciting that faint scratching sound that had drawn her in earlier.

"Look, Stone's not a bad guy. Big-time slacker, sure, and generally useless, but he's not mean or cruel or anything. And he does love his dad and his sister. I have a hard time believing he's the one who killed Chip, or that he'd let Daisy go down for it if he did." He shook his head. "At the same time, the fact that he's running can't be good. And if there's a chance this'll help clear Daisy, I'm willing to take it."

Hunter considered that for a second before finally giving a terse nod. "All right. So where are we going?"

"This island has two halves, basically," Cookie answered, happy to break in and possibly defuse the clash of manly egos filling the car with testosterone. "There's the part you've seen already, the nice, quiet little town of lobstermen and a few small shops. But then there's the other side. It's an artists' colony. According to some of the sites I read before we moved here, it got started back in the 1880s when a few Maine artists who'd done well for themselves purchased the northern edge of the island and started inviting friends out to summer with them. It's private property, but anyone can apply for a summer residency. If you get accepted, you get your own cabin for the summer, and I think they cover some of the meals, too. You just need to get out here and spend your time painting or drawing or whatever."

She saw Dylan nod in agreement. "Yeah, it's been a real godsend for the island in general," he explained. "Our population more than doubles every summer, which means we sell a lot more food, souvenirs, and basic services. The money from the colony gets a lot of small businesses through the winter."

"And this helps us how?" Hunter asked impatiently. "Do we think Stone is hiding out in one of the cabins and, what, waiting for us to get bored and leave? Or head over to Hancock looking for him so he can sneak out once we're gone?"

"Not exactly," Dylan said. Even without looking at him, Cookie knew that he wore a smug expression plastered across his face. "The colony has its own dock. And during the summer months, the ferry detours over there on its way back to Hancock."

"Ah. So you think Stone is waiting to catch the ferry there, rather than where we'd expect him." Hunter nodded. "Smart. Provided he's got a way to signal the ferry and convince them to make that stop, even though it's still spring."

"Contacting them is the easy part," Dylan answered. "The ferry pilot, Captain Bob, always carries his cell phone in addition to having his radio on, and everybody on the island knows his number. It's handy if you're running late to make the ferry and need him to wait a few minutes, or if you're checking to see if some package you ordered is on its way over."

Cookie considered that. "So we can assume that Stone called him and that Captain Bob is making the extra stop to get him. We just need to get there before he takes off again."

"I'm working on it," Hunter growled, slowing to

navigate a twisty turn. "This isn't exactly the interstate, you know."

Cookie quieted down and let him drive. She wanted to twist around in her seat and study Dylan in order to gauge whether he'd really forgiven her yet or not, but decided against it. That kind of motion could distract Hunter, plus she couldn't allow herself to blatantly stare at him. Not in front of present company. Awkward. Instead she peered into the visor mirror, which only gave her a glimpse of Dylan behind her.

Until he shifted, looked straight at her reflection, and winked. A flood of warmth flowed through her, enough to make her squirm, and she did her best not to gasp or sigh or even cry in relief. Judging by that little gesture and the smile quirking his lips, he had indeed forgiven her. And while she didn't yet know what the future might hold for her and him, if anything, Cookie knew the last thing she wanted was for him to be mad at her.

Though a traitorous part of her mind couldn't help her next thought: *if he never gets mad, you can't make up afterward.* The heat of her blush on her cheeks made Cookie turn her attention to the road ahead, staring intently out at the hilly landscape and trying to catch the first glimpse of the artists' colony they were speeding toward. She ignored the faint, throaty chuckle she thought she heard from behind her, though her face flamed even more at the sound.

Great. This was not what she usually had to worry about when trying to chase down a suspect.

It was several more minutes before the property finally came into view. They'd just topped another low hill, and up ahead, Cookie spied the peaks of several small roofs and the glimmer of the ocean beyond. "Almost there," she murmured.

"Any sign of Stone?" Hunter asked. His eyes were fixed on the road itself. Fortunately, they hadn't encountered any other traffic—a definite advantage to living on a small island, and one where most of its inhabitants were either out on their boats well before dawn or walked where they needed to go—but the road itself was narrow and meandering enough to require his full attention. Especially at the speed they were going.

"Not yet," she admitted, scanning the area as they approached, the roofs now resolving into a staggered row of small cabins. She squinted, trying to see past them, and finally spotted a dark sliver against the sun-lit water. "There's the dock."

They reached the first cabin and zoomed past it, giving Cookie a better view of the dock itself—and a curse slipped from her lips. "Damn it!"

Because she could also now see a lone, bright-white boat on the water. The ferry.

And it was already heading away from them.

"The ferry beat us here!" she cried out. "Stone's getting away."

Hunter slammed on the brakes, throwing all of them forward as the muscle car ground to a shuddering halt. They all stared out at the water, the departing ferry clearly visible, and the whine of the diesel engines barely audible. It was too far away for them to make out Stone's car, but Cookie had no doubt it was on there.

Hunter pulled out his phone and scowled. "No service. We can't even get the sheriff to intercept him."

Cookie and Dylan both did the same and shook their heads. The cell tower obviously didn't reach the artists' colony.

"What now?" Hunter demanded. "He's on the boat. We lost him."

But Cookie wasn't ready to give up just yet. "Is there any way we can get another boat?" she asked, twisting around to face Dylan. "One of the lobstermen, maybe? They could swing around here and get us then take off after the ferry."

But Dylan was already shaking his head. "Even if you could convince one of them to leave his traps behind and come get you, they're no faster than the ferry is. And he's got a solid head start. By the time you got onto the boat, Stone'd practically be at Hancock already."

Cookie sagged, dismayed at the answer. But Hunter had perked up. "Did you say 'faster'?" he asked, grinning as he put the Mustang in drive and executed a squealing three-point turn before peeling off back the way they'd come. "Because I happen to know exactly where we can find a boat like that."

Cookie stared at her ex-partner, shock and delight warring within her as she realized what he meant. "We can't take that," she insisted. "It's not ours."

"It's not anyone's right now," he replied with a shrug. "And you know I can commandeer vehicles when in pursuit. That's exactly what we're doing." His grin widened. "Besides, think of it as poetic justice. We're going to use the victim's own boat to catch his killer."

Cookie glanced back at Dylan, who shrugged helplessly. Whether he knew what they were talking about or not, it was clear he figured he was just the hired help. The decision was up to Hunter—and Cookie.

And Cookie found herself agreeing with her ex-partner. Maybe there'd be a few hard questions later, but if Hunter was willing to face them, so was she. Besides, right now it was their only chance to catch Stone.

"One problem," she offered as they finally screeched to a halt several minutes later, right back where they'd begun, at the very start of the island's main dock. "I don't suppose you know how to pilot one of those things?"

Hunter was already hopping from the car, and Cookie quickly followed, as did Dylan. "Me?" Hunter replied with a laugh as they sprinted toward slip number eight and the fancy speedboat sitting there waiting. "Not a clue. You?"

Cookie threw her own laugh back at him. "Yeah, right. I can swim just fine, but boating? That's a little beyond me."

Dylan, however, had lengthened his stride, and passed both of them. "Cast off the mooring lines," he ordered as he hopped onto the *Wins Low* and headed straight for the pilot's seat. "That's the two lines holding us to the dock cleats."

Cookie's eyes widened as she watched him reach under the dash and yank out a handful of wires. With a knife in hand, he went to work, obviously an expert at hotwiring. There was no doubt about it, eventually she was going to get his backstory. One way or another, she had to uncover the secrets of Dylan-the-handyman.

"Get the lines," he barked again, not even looking up.

"Roger that," Cookie called back, pointing to Hunter. "You get that one. I've got this one." And, stooping, she bent to pick up one of the boat's ropes, which hung loose in her hand. It had been tied to a cleat before, but that was the one they'd taken to Dr. Delgado. The one they suspected had ended Chip Winslow's life.

"Cheater," Hunter accused but quickly took care of the other rope as she clambered aboard after Dylan. He already had the engine going, and as soon as Hunter's feet thudded onto the deck he steered them away from the dock and out onto the open water. The throttle slammed down in its housing as Dylan opened it up to a high speed.

"We've got two things going for us," he yelled over the wind as the speedboat raced across the water. "First, the ferry had to swing out of its normal path to get Stone. It'll take them a little extra time to get back on course."

"And the other?" Hunter asked as he joined them by the controls.

Dylan grinned. "This thing moves like a bat out of hell." He gunned the engine, causing the boat to leap forward and send Hunter stumbling backward. "Might want to grab a seat."

Hunter glared at him but did as instructed. Cookie had grabbed hold of a conveniently placed handle to one side of the dash, and after briefly considering, she opted to stay there rather than seek one of the comfortable chairs set farther back on the deck. She could sit later, on the way back. For now, she wanted to be on the lookout for Stone and the ferry.

It didn't take long. Only a few minutes later, she stiffened and pointed off to the side. "There they are!"

Dylan nodded and brought the boat around with a deft flick of the wheel. He clearly knew what he was doing. "Do you want to wait until they reach Hancock?" he asked, "Or are we trying for an intercept?"

"What would that involve?" Hunter asked, rising from his seat to join them up front again.

"This boat doesn't have any kind of grapple," Dylan answered, "nor do we have a megaphone like the Coast Guard uses. So the best we could do is radio Captain Bob then pull alongside and jump across."

Hunter was already nodding and reaching for the radio, "Let's do it. Get me the ferry."

Dylan twisted a dial by the radio. "You're all set."

"Island Ferry, this is the FBI, do you copy?" Hunter

asked, speaking into the radio's handheld. "Over."

After a second of static, they got a reply. "This is Captain Bob of the Secret Seal Ferry. Did you say FBI? Over."

"That's right," Hunter responded. "I'm Special Agent Hunter O'Neil of the FBI. We have reason to believe you have one Stone Harris aboard. He's wanted for questioning. Requesting permission to come aboard and apprehend him."

The pause was a little longer this time, but finally Captain Bob answered. "This is for real?" he asked. "You're not just funning me?"

"One hundred percent real," Hunter assured him.

"Well, all right, then," the ferry captain said. "I'm guessing you're in that fancy speedboat that's racing toward me?"

"We are."

"If you can pull up alongside, he's all yours."

"Thank you." Hunter put the radio back on its holder and nodded to Dylan. "Let's go get him."

Dylan's only response was to race the engine again. But this time Hunter had braced himself beforehand and didn't move even an inch.

CATCHING THE FERRY proved to be the easy part. Jumping across to it from the speedboat was a bit more harrowing. "Can't we get them to stop?" Cookie asked, contemplating the water rushing by beneath the narrow gap between the two boats.

Standing beside her, Hunter shrugged. "We could ask, but I think we're testing the pilot's patience as it is. Come on, it's not that bad." He smirked at her. "You could always stay here."

"And let you make the collar on your own?" Cookie snorted. "Not a chance." Then, before she could stop to think about it anymore, she climbed up onto the speedboat's lip, balanced for a second, and jumped.

The impact of her landing radiated up her legs, but she kept her feet, straightening and turning to grin right back at Hunter. "Nothing to it," she reported. "Come on, scaredy-cat."

"You're impossible," he told her but followed her across easily. Then he surprised her by turning to look back at Dylan, who was still on the speedboat. "Thanks. We've got it from here."

Dylan frowned. "You sure?" he asked, directing the question more at Cookie than Hunter. "You don't need me to take all y'all back?"

But she shook her head. "He could have evidence in his car," she pointed out. "We'll need to bring that back as well. But thanks." She sent him a wide smile, letting him know just how much she appreciated his help, and the smile he returned was warm enough to make her feel flush again.

No question about it, Cookie thought as Dylan tossed them a quick salute and pulled the *Wins Low* away from the ferry. Dylan Creed was dangerous. To her, anyway. But it was a good kind of danger. Shaking off such thoughts, at least for now, she glanced around her. And had to laugh.

There was only one car on the entire ferry. A battered old Subaru. And, standing in front of it, frozen in terror, was one Stone Harris.

"Stone Harris," Hunter barked, crossing the distance quickly, his pistol in his hands and trained on the attempted fugitive. "I'm Special Agent Hunter O'Neil of the FBI. You are hereby under arrest for the murder of Chip Winslow. Get on your knees, and place your hands on your head."

Stone stared at the gun for a split second, then at Hunter's stony face, before doing exactly as he was told.

Hunter kept the gun pointed at Stone as Cookie sidled around the stoner and grabbed the zip tie Hunter handed her. The tie hummed as she secured Stone's hands behind his back. She nodded to her ex-partner once it was done and couldn't help grinning as he lowered the gun. It was just like old times.

After Hunter read him his rights, she hauled Stone to his feet, propelling him in front of her as she followed Hunter to the ferry's cabin. She'd seen Captain Bob a few times—most recently on their trips to the medical examiner's office—and the short, stout, graying ferry pilot looked the same as always, if a little confused by the recent events.

"Captain," Hunter started, pulling out his badge and ID and showing them to the man. "I'm Agent O'Neil.

Thank you for your assistance." He frowned then glanced at Cookie. "What do you think? Take him back to the island, or just question him in Hancock?"

Cookie considered it. "Might as well just do it in Hancock," she said finally. "We're already most of the way there. I'm sure the sheriff can accommodate us, and this way Captain Bob doesn't have to turn back around."

Hunter nodded. "All right. I'll call the sheriff and let her know we're coming. We can have her meet us on the docks to bring Stone in, and then one of us can drive his car over, or have a deputy do it."

"Sounds like a plan," Cookie agreed. She studied Stone, who was slumped in a corner of the cabin, the very picture of dejection. At last they would get some real answers.

22.

THE SHERIFF'S STATION in Hancock was very similar to the one on Secret Seal Isle except that it was bigger and had more staff—Sheriff Watkins herself, two deputies, and a woman who worked the front desk and answered the phones. "Make yourself at home," the sheriff told them when they arrived on her doorstep, Stone in tow. "Always happy to cooperate with our fellow agencies."

"Thank you," Hunter told her, ignoring the blatant look of lust the sheriff was giving him. Cookie hid her smile of amusement. Watkins seemed like a nice lady, and organized, but she was short, stocky, and middle-aged, with a bun of graying brown hair and features more appropriate to a kindly but firm grandmother than a sheriff. Not exactly Hunter's type.

Hunter had explained Cookie's presence as his employee once again, and no one had batted an eye. But the fact that she was FBI, even if on leave, meant that there wouldn't be any issues with the paperwork should it come into question later.

The office boasted several interrogation rooms, and she and Hunter hauled Stone into one of them, setting him down in a chair and claiming seats across from him. Stale smoke seemed to breathe from the walls as if they were thrilled to have an occupant. The dust on the table told Cookie it had been a while.

Hunter and Cookie shared a glance and mentally debated whether to leave him bound, Cookie urging leniency with soft eyes and Hunter pressing for sterner measures through his lowered brow. When he finally sighed and nodded, Cookie knew that she'd won, and she tried not to smirk as she freed Stone's hands. The used zip tie landed with a metallic clunk in the empty trash can.

"Thanks," Stone muttered, massaging each wrist in turn. "I was starting to lose the feeling in my hands."

"Sorry about that." Cookie leaned across the table. "Now that we're all here and unencumbered, let's talk. About Chip Winslow."

But apparently her act of mercy only earned her so much, because Stone huffed and looked away. "I've got nothing to say," he replied.

Cookie glanced over at Hunter, inviting him to step in through a single raised eyebrow.

Her ex-partner nodded and rose to his feet. "Listen, Mr. Harris," he began, pacing behind Cookie. Stone's eyes were drawn to the motion. "Let's put all our cards on the table, all right? Chip Winslow is dead. We know that he died from a blow to the back of the head."

Stone winced.

"We know that the fatal blow came from a dock cleat right by his speedboat, the *Wins Low*, on the island's main dock."

Another wince.

Hunter continued to pace, never taking his eyes off Stone. "We know that whoever killed him tossed his body into the water, hoping it would sink and disappear forever."

Stone was practically squinting now.

"And we know that the bricks used to weight the body down came from your family's lobster boat."

That one made his eyes widen instead, as all the remaining color drained from Stone's face.

"We also know," Cookie jumped in, "that Chip had an altercation with whoever killed him, late Saturday night or Sunday morning. And that Chip landed a punch but didn't take one himself." She studied Stone, particularly his face. Was that shadowing on the right side of his jaw the remains of a bruise? It was hard to tell.

"Given all that," Hunter said, "our top suspect is one Daisy Harris. Your sister." Now Stone was wincing again. The bricks were the only thing so far to have thrown him. Was that because he hadn't known about that detail or because he hadn't expected them to figure that out?

Hunter had stopped pacing and turned toward Stone, planting his hands palms-down in order to lean in. "Unless you want to see your sister go down for his murder, you need to talk to us. Now."

Stone stared up at him for a few seconds, his mouth working as if he was trying to speak or to cry but couldn't manage either. Finally, though, he turned away with a small sob. "Leave me alone," he whimpered.

"We can't do that, Stone," Cookie warned him, keeping her tone gentle. "Look, we're just trying to figure out what really happened here. I'd hate to see Daisy go to prison for something she didn't even do."

"She had nothing to do with this," Stone insisted, his voice shaking. He dragged one arm across his face. "It was an accident."

"An accident?" Both Cookie and Hunter moved closer to hear. "So Daisy didn't mean to kill him?"

"Daisy wasn't there." Stone lowered his arm to glare at them both. "It was me, okay? I'm the one who did it!" He'd half-risen from his seat during this declaration but now slumped back down, all defiance drained away. "I killed him."

Cookie met Hunter's eyes and inclined her head toward the defeated stoner. Hunter nodded and took a step back, giving her room to work. She'd always had the lighter touch of the two of them.

"Okay," she said, sitting back a little to give Stone some breathing room. "Walk me through it, then, all right?" She waited, but when he didn't reply she continued. "Look, Stone, just help us out here. We don't want to put you in jail. You said it was an accident, right?"

"It was," Stone insisted. He sighed and scrubbed at his face with one hand. "He'd been at the Salty Dog again, okay? Trying to bully my dad into selling the place. Dad said no, obviously. He loves that place like it was another kid. Daisy was working, and Chip hit on her. Like usual. The guy was pure slime."

Cookie nodded. "Daisy told us he hit on her all the time," she confirmed. "She also said she just blew him off whenever he did."

"Yeah." Stone studied his hands. "But it still pissed me off, you know? This is my sister we're talking about, and here's Chip oozing all over her. Gross." He shrugged. "So I gave him a piece of my mind. Told him to stay away from her, or else."

"Or else?" Cookie considered. Chip had been a decent-sized guy, and well built. Stone was a skinny little dude, no muscle to speak of. "Let me guess," she said. "That didn't go the way you'd thought?"

In the harsh light of the interrogation room it was impossible to miss Stone's sudden flush. "Jerk slugged me," he admitted without looking up. "Knocked me on my ass. Then he kept coming, rambling about how my whole family kept getting in his way and he was going to teach us some manners, starting with me." Stone was bright red as he continued. "I ran, or tried to, but I tripped over the bowline. It was dark. I couldn't see it. I was still trying to get my foot free when he came at me again."

Stone glanced up at Cookie, meeting her gaze. "I guess he hit the line too, 'cause next thing I know he's toppling toward me. I twisted and managed to get clear. He tried to grab at me as I rolled to my feet, but just missed me as he turned. He hit the dock hard, back of the head first. It made this sound like... like a watermelon hitting the floor and shattering." He shuddered. "I can still hear it."

Cookie felt for the guy, she did, but she knew it was important to maintain momentum, so she kept going. "So you guys tussled, Chip fell, he hit his head. Then what?"

"I was just going to get out of there," Stone continued, now staring off into space as he remembered. "But then I realized he wasn't moving. I thought he'd knocked himself out when he hit, you know? But his eyes were open. So I looked, and he wasn't breathing." He shook his head. "I—I knew he was dead. And I freaked." He raised his hands in defeat. "I mean, look at me. I've got 'lead suspect' written all over me. So I figured, he's dead anyway, but if I get rid of the body at least he won't take me with him." A small laugh escaped Stone then. "Guess I was wrong, huh?"

"What'd you do next?" Cookie pressed.

She needn't have worried, though. Apparently Stone had decided there wasn't any point in hiding anything anymore. "I wrapped him in a tarp and dragged him over to our boat," he told her and Hunter. "Took the boat out onto the water and, when I was far enough out, weighted him down with bricks then tossed him overboard. I figured either he'd sink to the bottom to get eaten by fish or wash out to sea, but either way I was good." He sighed and glanced at Cookie. "When I heard he'd washed up behind the inn, I couldn't believe it. All that open water, and he winds up right back on the island." He shook his head. "Unreal!"

Hunter leaned in with a question of his own. "Why'd you run?" he asked. "You knew we'd picked Daisy up. Were you really going to let your own sister take the rap for you?"

Surprisingly, Stone bristled at that. "No way," he snapped, showing more life than he had since they'd caught him. "I had a letter all written out, explaining what'd happened. I was gonna post it as soon as I was across the border to Canada. I'd never let Daisy take the fall for me. I was just hoping I'd have time to get away before I had to come clean." He looked around the interrogation room as if he was searching for a hidden camera. "Guess I was wrong, huh?"

"Where's this letter?" Cookie wanted to know. If he really had written one, it'd go a long way toward proving Daisy's innocence.

"It's in my car," Stone answered glumly. "In the glove compartment."

At a nod from Hunter, Cookie rose and exited the room. They had Stone's car keys in a box with the rest of his things, and they were cold in her hand as she snagged them before heading outside to the small station parking lot that doubled as the town's impound. Stone's Subaru sat there, and in minutes she had the door open, one of the deputies standing beside her as a witness. The glove compartment stuck, requiring some serious muscle, but when Cookie yanked on it hard enough, it flew open, spilling papers, old food wrappers, and other paraphernalia everywhere.

And right on top was a closed envelope that read *Hancock Police* across the front.

Cookie snapped a few pictures with her phone to record where the letter had been then scooped it up. She brought the letter back inside unopened and returned to the interrogation room. The deputy stayed with her all the way to the door. That way no one could later claim she'd swapped out a different letter or planted the whole thing in the first place.

"Is this your letter?" she asked Stone as she took her place at the table again and laid the envelope between them.

He nodded. "Yeah, that's it."

"Go ahead and open it," Hunter instructed. Stone did so, extracting a pair of pages covered in a scrawling hand. The papers fluttered as he held them. "Is that your handwriting?"

"Yes," Stone confirmed, his voice small, resigned.

"And is that what you wrote?"

Stone scanned the letter then said it was. Once that was done, Hunter spun the letter around so he and Cookie could read it.

It recounted exactly what Stone had already told them—he'd confronted Chip, they'd fought, Chip had fallen and hit his head and died, and Stone had tried to dump the body. Everything matched what he'd said, although the letter didn't explain that Stone had been running from Chip when he fell. But all the important details were there. Hunter shared a sharp, predatory grin with Cookie.

They had him.

23.

"WHAT DO YOU think will happen to him?" Cookie asked as she and Hunter rode the ferry back across. A deputy had given them a ride to the Hancock dock. Stone was still in jail there, awaiting his trial and sentencing.

Hunter shrugged. They were standing along the side, leaning on the railing and looking out at the water. It was just starting to get dark, streaks of color enlivening the sky, and there was a calm breeze blowing, pleasantly tangy with the salt from the ocean. As the air kissed her cheeks with its gentle caress Cookie realized it was moments like this that she was happy she and her mother had moved out here.

"Depends on his lawyer," Hunter answered finally. "If the guy's any good, he could argue that Stone never actually touched Chip, that he was the victim rather than the aggressor, and that Chip simply tripped and did himself in. Accidental death, with Stone an accessory at most and merely a witness otherwise. He'd get a slap on the wrist for obstructing justice by trying to hide the body, but that'd be it."

Cookie nodded. They only had Stone's word, of course, that Chip had tripped rather than been pushed, but they didn't have anything to prove it hadn't happened that way, which meant he'd have reasonable doubt on his side. Add to that the fact that Stone was a local, and although a miscreant, not an outright criminal, and that his father was a pillar of the community, she figured Stone stood a very good chance of being acquitted. It didn't hurt that nobody had liked Chip and that he was known to be a bully.

And she was fine with that outcome. They'd had plenty of cases back in Philly where they'd gone after real bad guys, unrepentant murderers and rapists and kidnappers, awful people who fully deserved to rot in prison—or in the ground. Stone wasn't one of those. Had he acted poorly? Sure, both when he'd tossed Chip's body and when he'd run from them. But he'd been trying to stand up for his sister. That had to count for something.

She'd believed him when he'd broken down back in the interrogation room. This wasn't a guy who'd set out to hurt anyone, much less kill them. Things had just gone badly, especially for Chip. But Cookie suspected, that whatever the District Attorney's decision, that night at the dock would haunt Stone for a long, long time.

MOISTURE FROM THE wet grass soaked her feet as Cookie and Hunter trudged back up the hill to the inn, and Cookie was surprised to see the front door open with all the lights on inside and music wafting out. It was her mother's typical hippie songs from the sixties, the same stuff she'd grown up on, but mixed in with the radio were women's voices, both loud and more than a little off-key.

Had Rain somehow talked Scarlett into singing? That boggled the mind. Because while Cookie's best friend had no shame when it came to her body or her words, she was convinced she was the world's worst singer and couldn't even be talked into doing karaoke in one of those private booths where no one outside can hear a thing. Heaven knew Cookie had tried convincing her enough times.

"Do we need to be worried?" Hunter asked as they climbed the front steps and crossed the porch. He was smiling when he said it, but he also had a nervous twitch to his eye, no doubt thinking about the last time they'd walked in on Rain.

Remembering that, and his reaction, Cookie couldn't help but giggle. "Don't worry, Scarlett's not her type," she assured him, leading the way. The voices were coming from the kitchen.

Stepping into the big, open kitchen, Cookie stopped and stared. Rain was there, singing as expected. But the other voice didn't belong to Scarlett at all. Instead the second singer was a heavyset older woman with long silvery hair and a lined face, bright-blue eyes, and a wide smile—a smile Cookie recognized at once.

"Winter?" she asked, dredging the name up from her memory. "What are you doing here?"

Winter Sage turned and beamed at Cookie. "Cookie!" She lumbered forward to wrap her arms around Cookie in a tight bear hug. "So good to see you, girl!" She hoisted Cookie off the ground, twirled her in a circle, and then set her back down again.

Hunter had followed her in and stopped at the doorway. "I take it you know this woman?" he joked.

"Yes," Cookie replied, laughing and trying to catch her breath at the same time. "She and my mom are old friends." She stared at the two older women. Was it her imagination, or did both of them look a little glassy eyed?

"That's right, Winter and I go way back," Rain agreed, turning from the oven with a tray of fresh brownies in her mitted hands. "Care for one?" she asked Hunter, offering the tray. "They're nice and hot." She and Winter both giggled.

Hunter was just reaching for a brownie when Cookie slapped his hand away. "He'll pass, thanks," she said, glaring at Rain. "FBI agents and brownies don't really mix."

"What?" Hunter stared at her as if she were crazy. "What're you talking about? I love—" He stopped speaking as his brain finally caught up with his eyes and ears and sent a frantic cease-and-desist to his brain. "Oh."

Winter, meanwhile, had gone as white as her namesake. "An FBI agent?" she managed after a second, plastering a smile back on her face. "How… interesting. And what are you doing up here, Officer? Will you be staying long?"

Cookie was studying her mom's old friend. "Will you?" she asked pointedly. Not that she didn't like Winter—she had fond memories of the woman teaching her to sing and to make gods-eyes when she was little— but she also remembered that Winter and Rain used to get up to all kinds of trouble back in the day.

"Oh, it's the most amazing thing," Rain answered, either oblivious to or ignoring Cookie's suspicions. "I was just sitting on the porch the other day, wandering around on the Web, and decided to see what Winter was up to. And would you believe it? She's in Hancock now. What are the odds?"

"Yes, what are the odds," Cookie replied. Suddenly her mother's suggestion that they consider Maine as a possible hiding place made a lot more sense. "And you had no idea she was here?"

Rain had always been good at looking innocent, so naturally she appeared to be a perfect angel, her expression completely neutral when she answered, "None whatsoever." But then she and Winter spoiled the effect by giggling like schoolgirls. Or baked college students left without adult supervision.

Cookie placed her hands on her hips. "Where's Scarlett?" she asked. "She was supposed to be keeping an eye on you."

"Oh, she's out back," Rain answered. "She needed a little rest."

That made Cookie frown even more. Scarlett was the type of person who could get up at five, run a few miles, make a brunch for ten, play hostess, clean up, head in to the office, defuse ten crises before lunch, conduct an international business meeting, balance the books, light up the room at a dinner party, map out a business plan that night, go to bed around one, and then get up the next morning and do it all again. And probably perform open-heart surgery and take down a drug cartel somewhere in there as well. The idea that she would be tired out from watching Rain cook was impossible to fathom.

Brushing past the two older women and leaving Hunter to decide his own fate, Cookie crossed the kitchen and stepped out the back door. Sure enough, Scarlett was lounging in one of the hammocks, one long leg dangling over the side to push off from the ground every time she swung back. She was also giggling and sucking on a lollipop.

"Scar?" Cookie asked as she approached her friend. Her eyes were full-on glassy. It was a wonder they weren't spinning like kaleidoscopes.

"Oh, hey, CJ," Scarlett answered, treating her to a huge, lazy grin. "How's it going? I've got the most amazing sucker—want a taste?" And she pulled the lollipop from her mouth, offering it to Cookie.

"No, thanks." Cookie frowned. She could already guess how this had all gone down. Rain had contacted Winter, who had come out on the ferry, conveniently after Cookie had already left. The two of them had started baking. Scarlett hadn't seen anything wrong with that. What could be more harmless than a pair of old friends getting together in the kitchen? So she'd left them to it.

And then they'd given her that lollipop. And maybe a brownie or two before that. Cookie and Scarlett had tried things back in college, and Cookie could tell from experience that her friend was well and fully lit right now.

Just then Rain appeared beside her. "Oh, you probably shouldn't have so much sugar this late in the day," she urged Scarlett, reaching out and snatching the lollipop right out of her mouth. Then she pressed a bottle of water and a bag of chips on Cookie's friend instead. "Here, try these. She's just tuckered out," she told Cookie. "She got up early to help us bake."

"Mom…" Cookie squeezed her eyes shut as she tried to keep from exploding. "Mom, what are you and Winter up to?"

"Oh, you'll love this," Rain answered, clapping her hands together, her eyes sparkling. "We're starting a new business. Baked goods and lollipops. We'll make a killing."

Cookie eyed the half-consumed lollipop in her mother's hand. It was a creamy brown, like caramel or dolce de leche—but were those green specks in it? "What kind of lollipops?" she asked.

"They're all-natural," her mother replied. She noticed Cookie's gaze and shoved the sticky candy into the pocket of her apron. "Very healthy. Winter has a medicinal tea shop, you know. We'll sell the goods out of there. It'll help make up for our lack of renters."

"You mean the renters you drove away by smoking pot with them?" Cookie sighed. "Mother…"

Winter stuck her head out of the back door. "Next batch is ready to go!" she hollered. She was clutching a large glass jar filled with some sort of green herb.

"Ooh, is that tea?" Scarlett asked, also spotting the jar. "I'd love some tea."

"We'll make you a nice cup of tea, dear," Rain promised. "But not with that. That's for the brownies and cookies."

Scarlett pouted. "Why can't I have *that* tea?" she asked. "Can I just have one of the brownies, then? If it's already got tea in it?"

Rain glanced over at Cookie. "Probably best to cut back," she declared. "Too many sweets will spoil your appetite."

"Mom," Cookie said, catching her mother's arm as Rain turned back toward the house. "Where did that 'tea' come from?" She waved in the direction of Winter, who had disappeared back inside.

"What? Oh, we got it in a moving sale," Rain answered absently, shaking loose. "Just this morning, when I went to pick Winter up at the docks."

Something clicked in Cookie's head. "A moving sale? Was the guy who was moving driving an old Subaru?"

Now Rain was the one eyeing her suspiciously. "Why do you ask, dear?"

Cookie considered pushing the issue but finally sighed. "Never mind."

She'd never be able to prove that her mom and Winter had bought the pot from Stone on his way out of town. There was no doubt in her mind that was what was in the jar Winter had been holding. But she had been surprised to learn that the deputy who'd searched Stone's car hadn't found any drugs whatsoever. Good thing for Stone, too, since he'd have been charged with possession on top of everything else. So he'd seen a chance to clear out his cache, get rid of anything incriminating, and make some quick cash, all in one fell swoop.

And the fact that he'd sold it all to her mother was just one more of life's little ironies.

Cookie trailed after Rain, and when she spotted Hunter, still in the same place by the kitchen door, he met her gaze and shrugged. *What can I do?* He asked with his eyes. He clearly knew what was going on here. He wasn't an idiot, and the brownies had a distinctive smell even amid the regular scent of fresh-baked goods. But he also obviously didn't want to admit to it, because if he did he'd have to arrest Rain and Winter and maybe even Cookie and Scarlett as well. And nobody wanted that. So for now he was just pretending to be unaware.

Which Cookie appreciated. She wished she could ignore it all so easily herself.

24.

TWO HOURS LATER, Cookie was sitting on the porch when Hunter emerged to join her. "All packed?" she asked without looking his way.

"Yeah, didn't really take much," he answered with a chuckle. That was true enough. He'd worn his one suit when he'd arrived and had brought along only a single duffel bag with, she assumed, clean shirts, ties, socks, running pants, and underwear, plus the usual toiletries. He was still wearing the pullover and slacks he'd gotten from the medical examiner, which meant he'd shoved his desperately-needed-to-be-dry-cleaned suit into the bag as well.

"I guess you need to get back," she continued, and it wasn't a question but a statement—one they both knew the answer to.

He answered her anyway. "I do, yeah." He sighed. "It's not like this was an official assignment, so this case of yours just cost me a week of vacation."

"Sorry about that." She did turn to look at him then.

"I really am glad you came up, Hunter."

"Hey, you know you can always call on me," he replied, reaching out to brush a strand of hair back from her face. His hand lingered there, stroking her cheek, and she shivered slightly, tilting her head so that he cupped it, enjoying the warmth of his touch. "Come back with me, Charlie," he urged then, his voice deep and rumbling. "You don't belong up here."

"There's a reason I took an extended leave from the FBI, remember?" she reminded him. "Nothing is resolved with DeMasi. Why would I go back now?"

He leaned in, his eyes black as the night. "Me." It was a tempting offer. Cookie had spent the last few days reliving the life she used to have. The excitement of uncovering clues, the thrill of bantering theories back and forth with Hunter, and the hum of—and dare she say it?—sexual desire that happened whenever Hunter was close. His gaze drew her in, warming her from the inside, and all she could see were his eyes, his face, his lips as they parted slightly, drawing hers to them like a magnet, pulling her closer—

The thud of feet on the porch steps made her startle and pull back reflexively, glancing about, as if she'd just been shaken awake.

And there, approaching them, was Dylan. Dylan of the sly smile. Dylan of the lean, wiry build. Dylan of the steel-blue eyes that sang with all the freedom of the sky. Dylan of the life she'd chosen and wasn't ready to give up without a fight. The man made her feel safe and wanted and admired and respected all at once. Even though they'd only known each other a week, and the strangest of weeks at that.

"Hey," he said, nodding at Hunter before turning those blue eyes on her. "Can I talk to you a sec?"

"Uh… sure," she managed. Hunter took the hint and rose to his feet.

"I'll be in my room if you need me," her ex-partner told her as he turned to go, the words heavy with invitation. He brushed past Dylan without making contact, which was a welcome change, and disappeared into the inn.

"Sorry about that," Dylan said as he took Hunter's vacated seat. "Guess I interrupted something?"

Cookie had to think about that for a second, forcing her sluggish brain to shake off all her conflicting emotions so she could think clearly. "Maybe," she finally admitted. "But I don't think so." She focused on the man in front of her right now. "What's up?"

He glanced away as if uneasy, then resolutely faced her. "I'm sorry about being such a dick the other day," he said. "I was worried about Daisy and angry at you for not telling me what was going on, but that's no excuse."

She shook her head. "It's fine," she assured him. "I get it. You were just looking out for her."

"Yeah, well, seems so were you," Dylan countered. "You were right about Stone and about going after him. And I know you were only doing what you had to with Daisy. I shouldn't have been a jerk about it."

Cookie wanted to assure him again that it wasn't a problem but could see that wasn't the reply he needed. Instead she just said, "Apology accepted," and offered her hand.

That made him laugh. "That's what I get now, a hearty handshake?" he asked with some of that mischievous gleam he'd had that first day they'd flirted right there on the same porch.

"What did you want?" she volleyed back. And held her breath, awaiting his reply.

He didn't keep her in suspense. "As much as you're prepared to give me," he answered bluntly, his eyes intent on hers, his face serious but not stern. Just focused. And interested. Very interested.

"I…" Cookie tried to reply to that but found she didn't know what to say. Crickets chirped in the night like a time bomb as she left her words hanging.

"It's okay. I get it." Dylan gestured toward the inn's front door, the way Hunter had gone. "I know you've still got some other stuff going on. So I'm just going to put this out there." He paused for a second then said, "I'm interested. In you. If you're interested in me, let me know. But only if you've straightened everything else out first. I'm not the type of guy to go after somebody else's girl or to get in the way of something that started before I got there." He rose to his feet without a sound, nodded at her, and then turned and made his way just as silently off the porch and into the night.

Cookie watched him go, marveling at his stealth, his

grace, and the way he threw her for a loop. Then she collapsed back into her seat with a moan. Even after moving out to the edge of the world, her life was never dull.

"WHAT AM I going to do?" she demanded a little while later. She was in Scarlett's room, perched on her best friend's bed, and the wall was hard against her back as she hugged her knees to her chest.

Sprawled beside her, Scarlett laughed. Cookie's best friend had recovered from her pot break, though she was still a bit wiped out. "Do?" she asked now. "You mean about the two hot guys literally fighting over you, or about whether to stay on this crazy-ass little island or come back to civilization?"

"Both," Cookie admitted. "I think they're pretty much one and the same, don't you?"

"I suppose." Her friend propped herself up on one arm so she could stare Cookie in the face. "What do you want to do?"

"That's the problem," Cookie replied, groaning. "Part of me wants to say 'to hell with all this' and chuck it and head back to Philly. See if I can get reinstated, partner with Hunter again, pick up the pieces of my old life as best I can, and then soldier on."

"And partner with Hunter in another way, too?" Scarlett asked, earning her a swat.

"But the other part of me," Cookie continued, "says

to stay here." She glanced around the room and out the window at the view of the water. The moonlight made the waves sparkle like tiny diamonds as they reflected the beams. "It isn't really all that bad, is it? There are some nice things about being here, and I'm not just talking about how the threat from the DeMasis has all but disappeared since we got here." She sighed as she found she couldn't stop watching the ocean. "And it is pretty."

"It?" Scarlett shot back. "Or him?"

Cookie tried not to giggle as she broke free from the sea's hypnotic trance, but the impish grin on her best friend's face did her in. "I suppose," she confessed. "It isn't just that, though."

"Good, because if it was, I'd have to slap you," Scarlett warned. "You are not throwing your whole life away after some dude, no matter how hot. Decide what you want and where you're more likely to get it." She grinned. "Then go out and get it."

After thinking about that for a minute, Cookie slid off the bed and rose to her feet.

"Where're you going?" Scarlett called out as Cookie left the room.

"I'm going after what I want," Cookie shouted back. Then she headed up the stairs toward her room—and the one other bedroom up there.

"Hey," Hunter said as he opened the door to her knock. He was back to his morning run attire, the T-shirt and yoga pants clinging to his muscled frame in all the right places. Cookie had to force herself to drag her eyes back up to his face. "All better now?"

"Kind of," she agreed. "I just needed to get a few things straight in my head."

She studied her ex-partner once again. Hunter was good-looking, smart, sexy, confident, compassionate, competent—everything she could want in a guy. Except stable.

Because while he was totally into her right now, that wasn't a sure thing. Hunter loved the thrill of the chase, but he didn't have a lot of follow-through. And he definitely didn't do entanglements and complications— or, as most people called them, relationships.

If she went back to Philly, she'd be right back in the same situation she and Hunter had had been in before she'd left. Both into each other but neither willing to commit, and Hunter not interested in anything long-term, while she wasn't going to consider anything fleeting.

And that was something neither of them was willing to change. Which was why Cookie could now steel herself to say, "Thanks again for everything, Hunter. Have a safe trip back, okay?"

Then she turned on her heel and walked away. She only went as far as the first floor and then the porch. But once she was out there she pulled out her phone and dialed a number. Those crickets were still chirping, but instead of a ticking time bomb, they sounded more like the beat of her heart.

"Dylan?" she asked when he picked up. "It's Cookie. I think I still owe you the second half of our first date."

And she grinned, then laughed, as she listened to his response.

Yes, she could definitely get used to this.

Find out more about Lucy Quinn's latest release at
www.lucyquinnauthor.com

Secret Seal Isle Mysteries
A New Corpse in Town
Life in the Dead Lane
A Walk on the Dead Side
Any Way You Bury It
Death is in the Air
Signed, Sealed, Fatal, I'm Yours

Lucy Quinn is the brainchild of New York Times bestselling author Deanna Chase and USA Today bestselling author Violet Vaughn. Having met over a decade ago in a lampwork bead forum, the pair were first what they like to call "show wives" as they traveled the country together, selling their handmade glass beads. So when they both started writing fiction, it seemed only natural for the two friends to pair up with their hilarious laugh-out-loud cozy mysteries. At least they think so. Now they travel the country, meeting up in various cities to plan each new Lucy Quinn book while giggling madly at themselves and the ridiculous situations they force on their characters. They very much hope you enjoy them as much as they do.

Deanna Chase, is a native Californian, transplanted to the slower paced lifestyle of southeastern Louisiana. When she isn't writing, she is often goofing off with her husband in New Orleans, playing with her two shih tzu dogs, or making glass beads.

Violet Vaughn lives in coastal New Hampshire where she spends most mornings in the woods with her dogs, summer at the ocean, and winters skiing in the mountains of Maine.

Made in the USA
Middletown, DE
25 July 2019